I0626756

the
fabulist

a novel

by
samuel w. reed

the fabulist

Reed Press

ISBN: 978-0-9990677-2-7

Copyright © 2017 by Samuel W. Reed

Cover design © 2017 by Reed Press

Cover photo by Florence Lilly

Printed by KDP Press

All rights reserved. No part of this book may be reproduced or used in any manner without the express written permission of the publisher.

This is a work of fiction. Names, characters, businesses, places, and events are fictitious. Any resemblance to actual persons, living or dead, is purely coincidental.

Dedicated to everyone who lifts me up.

I couldn't do this without you.

the
fabulist

1

Sunday

I tell her I'm on vacation. Vacation sounds more like *adventure*. Work is like... well, you know what it's like. Fuck. Work's not sexy. Adventure is sexy. Everyone likes adventure. She does. I can feel it.

She smiles out of the corner of her mouth as she places a cocktail napkin atop the bar, and then my drink. The sweat from the cold contents within beads up on the glass, soaking up and sticking to the napkin beneath it for dear life the same way her t-shirt clings to her torso on this hot, muggy night. I put the Mai Tai to my lips and imagine it's her... Mmmmm... So cool... *Refreshing*... And I watch over the curved rim of the glass as she greets her next patron further down the bar.

It's usually dead this time of year, but something's different now. Maybe it's her. Or maybe it's the convention of sales morons who mill about aimlessly when they're not in session or not taking up more than their fair share of the barstools at this overcrowded establishment. Or perhaps it's the busload of Japanese tourists I saw unloading from the pineapple airport earlier this afternoon, now wandering the resort looking for all the designated smoking areas in preparation for any unpredictable nicotine fits they might succumb to, I can't be sure. What I am sure of is that I picked this hotel because they pride themselves on privacy. They claim it's the quietest hotel on the island. It says so right on the website. And last year it was. Yet here I am, standing in what is quickly becoming the deep end of a pool of shouting corn-fed fraternity boys and I can't turn around without drowning in a sea of red jersey material and white stenciled numbers.

All I see are numbers circling me afire, and mouth breathers screaming at a small man in a matching jersey and a helmet running across a field of green plastic, all displayed on a sixty-two inch LCD monitor like he is the last hope for this nylon sect of the human race, legs outstretched, arms tight around an unseen object, no doubt something precious, sacred to human existence, like the Cup of Christ or a Dead Sea Scroll or something of monumental importance, racing onward in a swift display of athleticism and masculinity, up until that moment when he's blindsided by an opponent and dropped to the turf with a heavy blow and a raucous cheer from the other colored team. The corn-fed folk go wild over this, screaming and spitting in each other's faces. This must be what hell looks like.

*   *   *   *   *

The island hosts the basketball tournament every year, but the teams can only come out every five years or so, like the Olympics, or the World Cup, or something like that, which is great because it keeps the number of cornhusks from the mainland down from year to year, and away from quiet establishments such as this. At least it used to. I had heard rumors, like drips from a leaky faucet, that the tournament

would grow from eight teams to twelve, or was it sixteen, which would certainly explain this asshole she just served down the bar with Greek letters stitched across his chest like he's celebrating the proliferation of Latin by doing keg stands with all of his meat and potato friends.

My insecurities surge through me and I pause to take a deep breath. I shouldn't let him bother me. I've got a decent stipend and nothing to do for the next four days but watch college-age children compete in sporting competitions, so I pick up my glass and knock back everything but the ice and flash my winningest smile down the bar until at long last she glances my direction, and like a light switch turns on inside of her, she grins.

"That was fast," she notes.

I can't help but smirk. "Long day."

"You fly in today?"

"No." I say it so convincingly I almost believe myself.

She swipes the glass away like a card dealer collects cards. Swiftly. Neatly.

"You ready for another." She delivers the question as a statement, as if she's insinuating that now is my only chance to convene with her, and if I don't, I may never get the opportunity again.

"Why not?"

She holds my gaze for a moment of consideration, then snaps another low ball from a clean rack, and quickly splashes it with ice, light rum, Curacao, pineapple, grenadine, something I don't recognize, and the topper, my favorite, Myers dark. I could drink my weight in the stuff, and quite possibly have over time.

I spent an entire week in Jamaica a couple years back covering a championship for the Caribbean Basketball Confederation and I fell in love with the local sugarcane while I was there. The darker the better, the sweeter the juice. I'd only been on a few of these junctions at that point, and I wasn't exactly sure what I was doing, or maybe *getting myself into* is a better way of putting it, so when I dipped my toes in I was extremely cautious... At first. But now, I've learned. Everybody else is doing it, so why the hell not? When in Rome, right?

She brings my new drink over, ice still clinking inside the short glass, not yet melted beneath the warmth of the liquor, and replaces the

11

soggy napkin with a dry one. She sticks the glass on top, and I reach for it, maybe a little too eagerly. The napkin clings to the glass as I draw it to my face, dangling there like a ship set to sail, and her smile widens beyond the quiet pleasantries of the norm to a point of real expression. Intrigue and desire, I'd like to think.

"Long day indeed," she quips.

I try to respond, with quick lips and quick wit, my own smile widening to match hers for instinctual reasons I can't explain, but that asshole down the bar screams at the TV like a General to his unruly army and before I can retort she turns around, back to the bar, her back to me, back to her limes and her lemons, her maraschino cherries and blackberries as she arranges the sweet berry flesh into the garnishment tray. I set my glass down, defeated, and look around at all the hopeful and optimistic beer-bellied nylon jerseys that surround me.

Long day? *Who am I kidding?* It's gonna be a hell of a long week. Just thinking about it gives me heartburn.

I peer over the glass, sneering at the crowd as I swill the Myers off the top before it drips complacently to the bottom of my drink and loses potency. A quick slug of tart squeezed lime stops me from downing the whole thing and I acknowledge the pungent blend of alcoholic refreshment with a receptive *"Whew!"*

I think they painted since last time I was here. Or planted something. It's definitely different. I mean, besides the noise. Besides her. I definitely don't remember her. She moves about the bar quickly, quietly, easily juggling multiple tasks at a time for her countertop full of deprived patrons. Tourists. Salespeople. Fans. Imbeciles. I stare with contempt at no one in particular. They all hate me. And I hate them, so I narrow my focus back to the petite wonder of a woman pouring libations behind the bar, who without the faintest hint of acknowledgment casts her eighty-proof spell over us all.

She's shorter than me. Much shorter, with a loose V-neck T and straight bleach blonde hair pulled up into some rat's nest on top of her head, and bright blueberry eyes, and tan leathery skin from too many days under the radiant sun. I'm trying to make out the logo on her designer grade poly-cotton blend when she catches me and I look away. My eyes dart for something else to focus on, landing on nothing in

12

particular, and I can only hope I moved in time. Though how long I had been staring I cannot totally be certain, as momentarily, all time has been lost. My gaze dances around the hut, slowly landing back on her as she resumes work, and I sit back and wonder what it would be like to peel away that rolled and knotted t-shirt from around her waist which barely exposes the dainty piercing in her belly which dangles over the soft flesh where women get that mysterious darkened line when they're pregnant, as well as the stamp on her lower back acknowledging what an independent, free-spirited young person she is. A slave to no one but her own misguided attempt to be unique. If I had the chance, I would roll that t-shirt up so fast, right over her delicate head and her soft lemon locks and I would drop it right in the muck under our feet and let it soak up the beer sludge clogging the drain on the slick bar floor as we stand over it and kiss.

A kiss, two lips touching, softly, then gathering breath and momentum like a steam engine plowing forward, opening only to absorb the moment between one another, slowly stealing away the breath of the other, as soft pillow pecks turn wet and slimy and arms curl around bodies like serpent's tails, constricting around one another until tensions peak and muscles stiffen.

My sugar-coated head grows cloudy with fuzzy passages of half-memories and unfulfilled desires left unspoken until now. Not in words, but in warmth and emotion does this feeling permeate me from my brainstem to my belly and into my feet, and like a star-struck child, toward the sun I gaze.

She's beautiful I whisper to myself. Maybe a little too loudly in my rum cloud haze, as the old man next to me smirks and smiles, granting me a 'good luck' wink before patting a five-spot on the bar and emptying himself off the stool and back across the lighted path to the bridge. It's dark now. How did that happen? The asshole's still here, still staring at the TV, but now it screams at him, and nearly everyone else is gone, and she's left wiping down the bar and handing me my tab and asking me if there's anything else I need.

"A lift?" I chuckle like I was trying to be funny. I'm trying too hard. I always sucked at being funny.

She made that last one really strong. I can feel it now. Not to mention I literally just wrote my room number on the ticket. Room 1352. The ink's not even dry. I hold the pen in my hand as evidence. This does not go unnoticed.

"Aren't you staying at the hotel?"

I smile, leisurely. I probably look hammered.

"Oh, right," I concede. I should ask her to come over. I think that's probably too forward, so I scribble something on the bottom of the tab that resembles my name and hop off the stool like the old man before me, only I trip, stumbling headlong into a bougainvillea planter. I grab the bougainvilleas for dear life and turn, and she's there, laughing at me, ear to ear, grinning with the widest smile I've ever seen. All teeth. And those starry eyes.

"Are you okay?"

"Yeah. Absolutely."

I stand, brushing the fallen petals off my shoulder and head. A flood of warm nervous energy storms my gut, rising into my chest, and flushes through my face, making my skin tingle from ear to ear.

"Alright. Well... Have a nice trip." She can't say it without snickering. I must be quite the show. I smile as demurely as I can muster.

"I intend to." And with that, I abruptly turn and leave.

I didn't realize it before, but I'm drunk. Dangerously so. And I'm not interested in going to my room. Not yet. I just got here. Besides, it seems early. I look around the quiet resort and consider my options. The tiki hut is surrounded by a pool on most sides, and a rock fountain on the other. A bridge over a narrow river leads to a winding path lit by small torches on either side, all of that lined with ornate little plants, of what variety I have no clue. The landscaping here is truly impeccable. Not a blade of grass is out of place. A warm breeze waves the palm fronds above, drawing my attention out the back lawn, all the way out to the darkened coast. It's only a few hundred yards to the water, and I can see a boardwalk down the ocean with more tiki lanterns leading the way. And with that, I decide to explore further.

The last thing I remember is her tender voice calling after me as I cross the bridge.

14

"Aloha."

*   *   *   *   *

I wake up the next morning face down in the pillows. There's sand in my bed. I hate sand. The way it sticks to you, in your hair, in your toes. Along the crevices in your socks and your shorts, and when you go swimming, God forbid, up the hairy part of your crack. Fucking sand. And it's fucking *everywhere*.

But it was soft last night. I remember that. Under my feet, the infinitesimal granules dripping like an hourglass between my fat stumpy toes to form a cool buffer between my hot soul and the calm harmonious earth. Those tiny granules packed so densely along the beachfront to create an impenetrable barrier for the overzealous waves to break against, time and time again. The cool night mist, spraying off the impossible waves, dampening my skin with the salted night air. And as the memories flood the shores of my mind I slowly remember everything. But most importantly, I remember her.

2
Monday

It's Monday. Fucking Mondays. I suppose they're slightly better when you wake up in Paradise, but the mindset's the same. Work. Always fucking Work. It never leaves you. The Assignment. That Stress. I've got a headache the size of Wisconsin and the only thing I can think about is Work while a throbbing blood vessel courses liquid hot magma through my temple, pumping an excruciating pain directly into my bulging skull.

Ughhhhh.

I forgo the morning shower to hit the breakfast buffet just as it closes and grab a cup of scorching hot, slightly burned cup of coffee and watch as the buffoons exit the hotel. The pre-game pinheads dance

around the lobby in numbered nylon jerseys. The sinister salespeople glad-hand one another with their gel heads and blown-out bangs. And the Tokyo tourists load their cameras and fanny packs and slender Asian selves into a row of tiny little short buses set to the eastern side of the remote tropical island until evening. Good riddance. Let me drink my coffee in peace.

"Excuse me," she says. I look up, finding not the soft friendly face I was hoping for, but another more indigenous, grouchy looking one. She has a vacuum in her hand, and when she speaks, I see her gold tooth.

"I need to vacuum. The buffet's closed."

She moves on, muttering unpleasantries under her breath, and as she plugs the machine into the wall and loosens the handle I realize that she wasn't asking permission, or even telling me to leave. She was merely warning me directly and abruptly that she intends to vacuum. Right fucking now. Customers be damned.

The vacuum blares awake like an electric hurricane sucking up everything in sight with a deafening whir. Everything except my headache. That vacuum *is* my headache. It's a cigarette boat on a cord. My whole head throbs to the pulsing sound of the beater bar across the carpet, and that Doppler scream of air sucking for all its might before it finally ingests a tiny pebble that rattles through the intestinal pipe.

I gulp down the rest of my coffee, accidentally scorching all of my taste buds along the way, and decide it's time to leave.

Back at the room, I turn on the shower and get in. I don't usually get migraines, but right now I feel like the soft fleshy part of my brain is vibrating against the inside of my skull like a jackhammer, plowing through a concrete shell, determined to succeed, however impenetrable. It must be all the stress from everything going on. Everything I've been trying to ignore for these last few years. All those little realities that slowly creep up on you about who you are and what you've become and how many more years you have left before your time is up. And I haven't been sleeping well, either. That never helps. Course, I haven't slept well in ages, so maybe that has nothing to do with anything.

It starts to get steamy and all the blood rushes to my head. I squeeze my eyes together to try and counteract the pressure against my temples, but nothing helps. I masturbate but halfway through I get bored and give up. Nothing can stop this pain in my head. I think of her and the way that t-shirt hugged around her waist when that bitch with the vacuum somehow pops into my head and I realize I have to pee. You'd think you'd be able to have more control over your own thoughts, especially in a moment like that, a particularly hot and steamy one sometime after her shirt had dropped to the barroom floor, but sometimes other shit just creeps on in. Like that gold-toothed woman with the vacuum. I pee in the shower, rinse off one last time, and step out. The glass shower door screeches in horror at my saggy overweight skin, so I slam it closed to teach it a lesson. The towel is nice and soft, with initials embroidered on either end in navy blue. I've already got two in my suitcase, plus a terrycloth robe and slippers.

I check out the minibar for the first time since I arrived and I'm surprised to find it competently stocked. High-end booze, beer, and prices. Excellent. Normally I wouldn't touch this thing, but here, right now, I have the stipend. It's the one decent thing about this whole damn gig, the stipend. I could live off the stipend alone for a month back home, probably longer even, but unfortunately, it doesn't work that way. Whatever's not covered by a receipt has to be returned. Charges for the airfare, hotel, food, transportation and anything at the games themselves are all covered. Even the booze. Plus, if I incur personal expenses after the stipend runs out I can add them to the expense report, as long as I have a receipt. Sometimes they accept it, other times not. I got a $400 massage at a spa in Houston once and wrote the whole thing off as stress therapy research. But when I tipped the shoeshine guy $10 at the airport they told me that gratuities were not covered by their policy. It didn't matter that the shoeshine itself was free. And that was one hell of a shoeshine, let me tell ya.

But here's the rub: I only get $250 a page. Sounds like a lot until you consider they only want three pages. Fifteen hundred words. That's seven hundred and fifty dollars, max. That's it. For a week's worth of work. And I probably won't book another one of these things for another month, if I'm lucky. This one, in particular, is a pretty cush

gig with a start-up pop culture mag that wants an "exciting, fresh take" on the growing popularity of the Tournament from "a fresh new perspective," which I can only assume is why they hired me, a middle-aged man with saggy teeth. I'm so *new* and *fresh*. Oh, what the hell. I'm gonna shoot for two thousand words and see what happens. See if I can get a full grand out of the deal. Maybe I can at least squeeze an extra hundred out of 'em, the cheap bastards. They don't send me on enough of these joints to make a living. But they send me on too many to do anything else. My last one was for their sister company, a fashion blog that paid me to follow around the Saints for a week to report on what they were wearing outside the locker room. A monkey could do my job. And I think in some cases they have.

  So here I am, alone again. This time in Paradise. With four fucking pages and a stipend. For one stupid tournament. And I could give a shit who wins. Honestly, I feel it's pretty obviously been decided: we're all fucking losers.

  Even still, I do like to dress up for the games. There's no reason in particular other than that I don't want to associate with *them*. You know the ones. The face-painters, the costumers, the overly obnoxious super-fans, the Greeks, the band members, the alma-maters, the season ticket holders, the average bum who just walked in off the street to beat the weather for a couple of hours and get a soggy kosher hot dog… They're all the same. I dress up so I don't get confused with them. Yet somehow, I look worse. I look even more desperate than they do, standing there in my suit and tie, staring at the team in a full-body sweat, not because I'm anxious about the game, but because this isn't the summer weight wool I thought I was bringing, but the pinstriped winter wool made to withstand the sub-zero temperatures of a football season in Chicago. But it makes me feel good to look this way. I feel important. The cabbie looked at me like I was the owner of the team. Of course, if I had been, I wouldn't have been riding in the back of his rat shit infested taxi. It smelled like they just slaughtered a pig in there for tomorrow night's luau. He had a ring of plumerias around his rearview and kept asking me if I'd been lei'd before breaking into an ear-shattering, high-pitched squeal of a laugh. He thought he was being funny. I've never wanted to punch someone so badly in my life.

No, I take that back.

The ticket taker wasn't much better. She kept looking at me like I was at the wrong convention. The sales thing is back at the hotel, I could feel her say, as she eye-rolled me through the turnstile. Maybe she's right. Maybe I should have gone there just to check it out. Fuck with some salespeople. Find somebody to fuck. Ah, what's the use? Security's got one hand down my pants and she's a quarter inch from grabbing the flask full of whiskey I shoved in my underwear before I wink at her, remove her hand, and slide on past. They don't give a shit. Rule of Life #1,391: If you look like you know what you're doing, then 99% of the time you'll get whatever the fuck you want. The problem is, these days everybody knows that, so 99% of the time you've got 100% of the dumbasses out there running around acting like they know everything.

Stupid statistics. Statistics are things stupid people say to justify shit they know nothing about.

I spend an inordinate amount of time in the bathroom washing my hands after the first quarter only to return to find my seat taken, so I usher myself to the back of the auditorium where I can no longer tell which jersey says Kansas and I've long forgotten which color is which. And they keep switching sides, which is confusing as all hell. I was much closer when I first got here, but it was so dizzying being on the floor like that I kept worrying I was gonna spill my flask all over that hard-polished wood, not to mention all those flashing cameras, and then I did spill my flask all over the hard-polished wood, and my pants, hence the trip to the restroom.

I can see the whole game from up here, well, except for the people. But from here the plays look like beautifully orchestrated dance routines between a symphony of acrobats comprised of tall gangly men and their ravenous screaming fans. And the scoreboard is right there. Freaking huge, with its blaring loudspeaker and microdot numbers counting down the seconds 'til doom... And a couple of hot girls squeal beside me, either in agony or ecstasy, as they root for number 7, who they seem to think is having a great game.

The next game isn't near as interesting. The hot girls are gone and my stomach is killing me after all the sausages and popcorn. Not to

mention I'm out of whiskey, so I wander back through this maze of a makeshift auditorium to find something to drink. Preferably alcoholic.

What the hell happened to this place? We used to put on sporting events in masterful coliseums, works of art in their own right. This place is a dump. It's basically a community rec center with a middle school quality basketball court. To somebody, this contest is life or death, but not to me. Only the latter. As I wander through the painted cinderblock halls, I consider the *actual* Coliseum in Rome, and all of our cheap, Americanized, plasticine versions on the mainland. Behemoth structures intent on forcing upon their eager patrons the same acrid, depraved acts billed as entertainment as centuries before: testosterone filled men competing with one another in a fanciful reenactment of war.

What is it about this culture, this species, this *life* that demands our constant exposure to entertainment and sports as a diversion from ourselves? What is this attraction meant to distract us from? And what is it about the magnificent, the majestic, and the spectacular that we are so drawn to that makes us invest in false heroes, celebrate false celebrities, and upend our entire lives for a glimpse of the gods that we have helped put on their pedestal? And for what? Why do we spend our hard-earned money from the fruits of our labors on fleeting experiences and worthless paraphernalia that only serves to remind us how ordinary and boring our lives really are? Why do we doom our mortal souls to the never-ending search for eternal happiness to begin with, knowing that once we get there the wallpaper will need to be redone and it will no longer be as good as it was in our heads because nothing ever is, so that, too, becomes a self-fulfilling prophecy for a life full of loathing and disappointment. And if that's all we get then what's it all for anyway? Why are we here and how did we come so far not to be anywhere at all? And what makes me think of this shit in the middle of a pissant, concrete building, inside of which if there were to suddenly be an unexpected earthquake I would be buried for the rest of my short endangered life.

With the walls caving in around me, all I can think about are the people. What we're made of. What we've become. I mean, the Romans fought tigers and shit. Bears, even. Each other if they had to, with

21

spears and swords and knives, anything they could get their savage little hands on. And here we are, lining up, tuning in, and idolizing someone who calls themselves a Lion, a Tiger, a Bear, or Cougar, or Jaguar, or Devil, or Demon… but all they do is bounce down a wooden lane, prancing atop the reflective lacquer, their rubber soles squeaking at one another like rubber duckies as they toss their precious leather ball between them until they can get it into the tiny metal hoop.

"Taxi!"

Within minutes of arriving at the hotel I'm back at the tiki hut, back at the barstool where I first saw her, back to trying to see if I can get her attention by offering a variety of smirks, smiles, and wide-eyed expressions to draw her attention, but it's no use. Nothing I say or do draws her my way. She's ignoring me for sure. I must have said something last night, something inappropriate perhaps when I didn't realize it. Or maybe it's all the staring? How can I be sure? I mean, I know the place is packed, but that's no excuse. Fucking gel heads and stiff bangs, goodie bags and cigar breath. It's only 4:45. The convention must have gotten out early. I'm lucky I got a seat. I size up the rest of the room, noting the diversity of age, race, and shirt material sandwiched together on this little isle of concrete cornered by the pool.

"Hey there."

She surprises me the moment I drift away. I don't like surprises.

"Hey."

"Another long one?"

I must look tired. Or worse, old and confused.

"Another long day?" she clarifies.

I stare at her blankly. God, I hate surprises. I wonder how old she thinks I look?

"You said yesterday that-"

"Right… Sorry…. Yeah. Another long day."

I'm a fucking rodent. I can't help but glance at her tits.

"Another Mai Tai?" She's not as assured of herself as yesterday. Maybe she's tired. Tired of a system designed to keep the wealthy elite in power while the poor pay for it with the days of their meager lives. Tired of a life where no matter how hard she works, she will always be judged by her appearance first, and then by her personality and skills.

22

And most prominently, tired of assholes like me, coming in here ordering complicated drinks, under-tipping, and over staring. She must be furious right now. I would be.

"That sounds great" I spout. I overcompensate, trying to be as chipper as I can.

"Just watch out for the bougainvillea," she quips, and to my delight, we maintain eye contact, and she smiles. That bright and beautiful smile. Her eyelashes flutter over blue irises in full bloom, and like a cheerful bunny she wiggles her nose and leans over to make the drink. She looks up and we make eye contact, and like children on the opposite sides of the elementary school dance floor, we smirk and turn away. It's as if we've already shared our most intimate secrets about ourselves, while we anxiously wait with eager anticipation to hear about the other. And then--

Some overgrown asshole bumps into me, shoving me halfway across the bar. I scooch my barstool over to accommodate him. Big mistake. Now he saddles up and makes himself at home, and as she sets down my drink, he's leaning in, screaming his order at the top of his lungs

"Can I get an *extra* dirty Grey Goose martini, and y'all got any of those olives with the blue cheese you can put in it?"

He knocks into my freshly made libation and dumps the whole fucking thing right down my shirt with the swoop of his elbow.

Goddamnit, man. I really like this shirt. *And* my jacket. And don't even get me started on these pants.

I turn to scold him with my best eat-shit-and-die gaze… but he's eight times my size, and his biceps are as large as my head, so I quickly register that tussling as an option no longer on the table and sit my scrawny ass right back in my seat. Fortunately for me, he's a real softy.

"Oh, bro, I am *so* sorry. Jesus. My bad dude. I… Shit. Let me get you a drink. Fuck. You want my shirt?"

And before I know it the ape's pulling off his shirt. I mean, really. I don't fucking need this right now. He's muscular, and tan, and all up in my business right now. Like, *seriously*.

"I'm fine."

Only in Paradise is that whole "No Shoes, No Shirt, No Service" thing, *not* a thing.

"Dude, I just dumped your grape juice all over you. I'm so sorry, bro-"

"It was a Mai Tai." Ab-Face Dick-lick Twat-Fucker.

"Bless you-"

"No." Asshole. "I said it was a Mai Tai." I slow it down like English is a second language. For me or him, I'm not sure.

"Excuse me, miss?"

She glares at him, a cruel and scathing glare. I love her.

"Can I get another High Tide for my friend over here? And you got any towels or anything I can use?" He points to the lake of sugar atop the bar as if she hadn't noticed.

"Sure thing." She looks at me, those big blue eyes enveloping me like a soft warm blanket. The next thing I know he's dabbing the ice out of my crotch with a green-striped hand towel.

"Are you sure you don't want my shirt?"

"Please. Get that away from me." My face doesn't have to say this because my arms are doing fine.

"Alright. Suit yourself. But if there's anything you need, I'm over there with my friends."

I turn, an empty gesture, just long enough to see that his friends are all snickering and pointing from the corner, the queens. My racing mind skips a beat as the gears grind to a halt and I turn back to face my attacker. He swivels back into his skin-tight shirt and grabs his martini off the bar, then he winks at me before skipping to his seat with the hip snap of a Latina salsa dancer.

Waitaminute.

Was that dude just hitting on me this whole time? Was that just a set-up? I glare incredulously at the laughing queens as they greet their fearless friend with giggles and back pats.

Imafuggingidiot.

She lands the refresher on a new napkin. It sticks, but not much, and I take a quick slug.

"I think he likes you."

My entire shirt is completely soaked.

24

"He has a funny way of showing it."

"Guess it really is one of those days."

"See, I told you. You can't make this stuff up."

She laughs. A real, honest laugh. God, those eyes. And those lips. The slightly pursed wet little pillows, the bottom one slightly dry with flaked skin and indented where she bites it, a nervous habit from all her anxious bunny energy, or maybe it's contemplative, as she holds her cards just narrowly out of my sight. Either way, she likes me, I can tell that much. If I can keep this going.

"You, uh…"

I trail off as words elude me. Any words. All the words. Out of my entire vocabulary, confronted with thousands of choices for creating depth and meaning and nuance so that this woman who I so clearly already adore will, too, find me appealing, funny, and endearing, I remember nothing.

"You work here long?"

Jesus Christ. That's the best I can come up with?

"Year or so. All over the hotel, though. Seven months on Tiki duty."

I nod as I take another drink. What am I supposed to say to that? Ask stupid questions, you get stupid answers.

"Cool." It's the best I can come up with.

"How about you? You out here for work?"

"No. Vacation."

"You said that." She laughs with that audible scoff like she sees right through me. I guess it doesn't help I'm practically in a tuxedo. I look down and I suddenly realize… Oh, Christ. I look just like *them*. The sales morons. I hope it's not a multi-level marketing thing. The look on my face alone gives my sudden realization away.

"It's not what you think."

It's really *not* what she thinks. But either way, I lied. How can she look past that now?

"And how would you know what I think?"

"I wouldn't… I just… Uh…" Words betray me once again.

She leans over the bar again. Arms folded in front of her, a curious expression crawling across her face. Impossible to read. I'm scared to even know. This woman is a mystery.

"What am I thinking now?"

And like that, she's got me. The rest of the world means nothing when she zeroes in her laser blue eye beams on you... And like a squirmy rat under the hot bulbs of her interrogation lamps, I squeal.

"I dunno." I'm like a teenage girl with a celebrity crush.

"Try." The way she looks at me defies meaning. It defies reason. I know if I disobey her, there will be consequences that I am unprepared to meet.

"Okay... You're thinking... That I can't be on vacation because most tourists only come in the summer... or spring break... and that this time of year the only people that come here are golf hacks or convention slugs, or they bought a Japanese destination package, or they're some sports super-fan or one of the teams associated with the basketball programs. And, judging from my attire alone, and process of elimination, there's a 70% chance I either coach a college basketball team or spent my day in a seminar learning about the best ways to activate and expand my business network."

She squints at me, a blank slate. Confusion, maybe? Interest? The longer I stare, the more I think it's disgust.

"That wasn't what I was thinking."

She turns.

"Oh really?" The words spout from my mouth with such defiance my own confidence astounds me. What am I even talking about with such authority, and why are the feathers on the train of my peacock's tail so haughty?

"Your elbow's getting wet."

She points at my arm, where a new puddle of rum has formed, missed in the earlier cleanup from my previous suitor, the Queen.

She takes a new towel, orange stripe this time, and wipes the spot up on the bar, then holds the towel ever-so-gently against my elbow, just to soak up any extra liquid that might not have soaked into my heavy wool jacket, which is most of it.

I look at her, and she smiles. My fears are unfounded. Her gentility and grace exhibited now so plainly. So explicitly. And in that smile, I feel my self-doubts melt away. And for the first time in a long time, my shoulders fall at ease, and I relax.

"So which is it?"

She's startled me again. My insecurities pique immediately. "Excuse me?"

"College basketball coach or sleazy sales guy?"

I buzz with excitement, the slow roll of the rum filling me with courage and witticisms until I practically gush with--

"Neither. I'm on vacation, remember?"

She looks at me carefully. I'm a mystery. I'm an anomaly. Something about me doesn't quite add up.

She smiles as she backs away and our moment is over. Duty calls. I'm lucky I got that much out of her. She was wiping the counter down the whole time. Funny how sometimes you miss the details, only to remember them moments later, perhaps slightly different than they actually happened. She's a good employee, I can tell you that. She takes real pride in her work. I hope they pay her well. Nobody could live off her shorted tips.

I sip from the Mai Tai and note it's even better than before. I don't know what she does back there, but she's a magician. A magician who's not alone. Someone else works with her tonight, most likely in rightful anticipation of the growing crowd at the hotel. It's a guy. *Ken.* Who cares about Ken? She's the real draw around here. She's an entertainer; cracking jokes, popping beer caps and bottle corks, and pouring drinks from multi-tiered liquor bottles all while she salt-rims glasses filled with freshly squeezed lime and Añejo tequila like she's the esteemed conductor of a liquor-soaked orchestra. And she sells the top-shelf stuff, too, only she keeps it on the bottom so she doesn't have to continuously use the stool or ask that guy Ken if he can reach it for her. She's so cute.

Ken looks like a douche. Ken asks me if I need anything as I sip the melted ice off the bottom of my glass. I tell him I'm fine. I'm waiting, just like the others. Like a vulture. My finger circles the rim of the glass in a slow crescendoing chime. It squeals to a stop when after

27

an excruciatingly long wait she turns to face me, finally unleashing those reflective moonbeams on yours truly, and I get to say...

Actually, I don't say anything. I just nod, because we're simpatico and she knows exactly what that means.

"Another?" she clarifies.

I nod again, to double the confirmation. Maybe we're not quite as simpatico as I think. So, I triple down.

"Please."

Ice. Rum. Juice. Juice. Juice. Something else. Myers. Cherry.

"Here you go."

"Can I get an extra cherry this time?"

She looks at me curiously. I don't even know what I just said. I think I'm flirting.

Then she grabs them, two long-stemmed maraschino cherries connected at the stem, which she holds from the joint and dangles in the air before she spears a cocktail sword through them, red syrup dripping from her fingertips as she drops them into my drink.

"Enjoy."

She licks the sticky red syrup from her fingers before wiping them on a towel and turns with a wicked grin. The little rascal. She's toying with me. She glances at me from the frozen daiquiri machine, then pulls the metal lever that makes the nozzle drool cold daiquiri goop all over the inside of the glass. Her hips sway to the flow of the daiquiri machine like it's an old R&B jukebox, and I look away, only I can't restrain myself for even a moment, and after a microsecond, I immediately glance back. She serves it down the bar to a gingerly old woman with a smile. *She probably does that to everyone* I consider as I polish off the last of my drink. Man, that was quick. Each one tastes even better than the last. That's the problem with these things, I quickly remember. These and margaritas. And long island iced tea, the way my mom used to make it. With simple syrup, and a heaping ton of fresh lemons & limes. That way it's sweet and citrusy and alcoholic as all hell. Delicious. I let the ice draw back in the glass and she shows back up, right on cue.

"Hey, I'm sorry, but I'm almost out of Myers. Can I get you something else?"

Record scratch. That is not what I was expecting. I turn the tables on her.

"Pick a shot. Then make two. One for me and one for you."

Oh, the horror. Did that Dr. Suessery really just escape my lips? I must sound like the biggest douche bag on the planet. I probably sound even stupider than Ken looks.

She smirks, quietly acknowledging I'm the queerest straight guy alive, before heading to the other end of the bar. At first, I figure she's calling the authorities. She's got her phone out and she's put herself in timeout, backed into a corner. Then, I see her sneak a bottle. Then another. Red. Brown. Round. Clear. What the fuck is she making? Then, to my amazement, and possibly chagrin, she brings over two low balls and sets them on the counter. They're filled to the brim with something that strongly resembles the color, clarity, and complexity of red cherry Kool-Aid.

"Those are the biggest shots I've ever seen."

"I know! Right!" She seems easily impressed.

Please don't make me drink this bloody red concoction, whatever the fuck it is.

"Please don't make me drink this bloody red concoction, whatever the fuck it is."

"You asked for it. Two red-headed sluts, my way or the highway."

"I am so afraid right now."

I actually say that. She laughs out loud and holds her glass in the air like 'You pussy, if you don't do this I'm gonna slosh this liquor all over your face," which I really don't want to go through again. I reluctantly pick up the glass, we cheer, clink our glasses together, each spilling red sticky liquid over the edge they're so full, and we chug. It goes down surprisingly smoothly. Refreshing even. She really is a magician. Either that or she already knows I'm a pussy.

"Wow."

"I know, right? It's good, huh?"

"Very."

She puts my glass inside her own and swoops them off the bar top and out of existence.

"You want to do another?" I'm desperate. I'm obvious. I shouldn't have said that.

She hesitates. She's got a lot of work to do. It's super busy tonight. Even busier than last night, but the crowd doesn't bother me anymore. After that game, I can handle anything.

Ken looks pretty mad at me right now. Fuck you, Ken.

"Just one," I prod again.

She hesitates, but not much. "Okay."

Next thing I know she's back in the corner, only I don't think she used her phone to make this round. It tastes good, either way. Like cherry Kool-Aid again, only brighter. More kick. We do three more rounds before she has to drag me off my barstool so she can cash out and roll down the rain cover that serves as a tiki shield after they close. Ken carts the last rack of glasses to the kitchen as Mena clocks out and I convince her to come with me to another bar. I must have turned on the charm or something because she agrees. Whatever it was, it clearly worked. Sometimes I can be funny when I'm drunk. Then again, I can get mean, too. But not here. Not in Paradise. Maybe I tipped her really well. I honestly don't remember. I'm just glad she said yes.

*　　*　　*　　*　　*

Her jaws snap a piece of watermelon bubblegum and all I can think is I could be her father. Well, only if I had a kid when I was, like, ten, but still. This should concern me, right? But the way she looks at me, with that all-knowing, other-worldly look, nobody has ever looked at me that way. Her soul is too old for her to be my daughter. Hell, she looks older than me. At least her wrinkled up, sun-dried raisin skin does. But those big baby blues stare up at me with that doughy grin and I just melt. I make her nervous though, I can tell. She sits across from me at a high-top bar table plucking the sequins off her t-shirt.

"Aren't those supposed to stay on there?"

She tries to act nonchalant about it, like she wasn't just picking the factory glued decoration off her favorite t-shirt, in effect ruining it, all because at this moment right now she doesn't know what else to do

with her hands, but the evidence lays in a sparkly pile on the unfinished wood table.

"Oh, right."

It's loud as shit in here. Between the hip 80's punk music blasting from the mini speaker overhead to the attempt of everyone in attendance to yell over it, my eardrums are under violent attack. We're in some sort of tiny tiki dive bar with fake bamboo on the walls and little black and white photos of the islands hanging from the nooks and joints in the hard plastic wood. I feel a warm glow across from me, gazing up at me in wonder, and my insides begin to flutter like a pale chicken ruffles his ivory feathers inside me, which sends shivers down my spine.

What is this sexual magnetism between us? Is it just me who feels it? Or is it both of us? Why haven't I ever felt it like this before? Or have I, just so long ago that I've forgotten the magic of that first spark, that early nervous excitement and heavy lusting that makes every nuance, every look, and every accidental touch spring to life and stimulate the senses in new and evocative ways.

My wife had that, I think. We were young. I don't remember anymore. It was a long time ago if she did. Before she left me. Back before she was attracted to another man. And like a magnet, that other man was attracted to her, and my negative electrons opposed her negative electrons until we eventually repelled each other so far away that we no longer come into contact, for as long as we both shall live.

It's so loud I can hardly think. Or rather, that's all I can do, because it's too loud to talk, so we stare. We smile. We break into laughter together over the simplest thing. A look. A glance. A reaction to some otherwise insignificant person that sets us off in unison, forever forging our bond in laughter and cherished moments we don't even fully understand. My mind reels just looking at her. Her soft lizard skin. Her deep blue eyes. They look dilated they're so big, and I lose myself in them time and time again. My head swims under her long curly eyelashes, and her soft supple lips. I could taste them. And her poly-cotton blend shirt... Wait... When did she change her shirt?

"Are you okay?"

"Me? Yeah. Why?" I hiccup.

"You look sick."

I feel sick. The entire room is spinning and everything is red like a Kool-Aid stained dream. I can't tell if there are actually colored lights in this screaming tiki hell or if my eyeballs are just filled to the brim with red dye #3.

"Oh. Sorry. I've had a lot to drink today."

"Do you want to go back?"

"I dunno. Do you?"

"Let's go back. I'll help you."

We walk under the stars as she guides me back from wherever we've been. The lights blur above and the frothy white line between the ocean and the sky vibrates to the vanishing point. Then suddenly, there's sand beneath my feet. It's even softer than before. Like cold silk, slipping between my toes. And she's next to me, holding onto my arm for dear life as I escort her down the beach. Or she, me. Whatever. A beer-like froth washes over our feet as we dip our toes into the cool Pacific water. The aroma of saltwater and rotten sea creatures wafts through the rank muggy air, and I feel queasy, like a young, green mariner aboard my very first vessel headed out into rocky seas, and I try not to yack all over her.

The next thing I remember is the sound of the bolt in the door sliding unlocked and falling into bed. The door clicked again and it was quiet.

3
Tuesday

There's sand in my bed. *Again.* And all over the cool tile floor. What is it with this place, anyway? Don't the maids ever change the sheets? Do they vacuum in here at all? Or after years of futile sucking and mopping, sweeping and dusting have they finally given in to mother nature's crystalline salute to time and said: "Fuck it?" I know I would.

My head is pounding. *Again.* There's a glass of water on the table. Next to the room key. Did I do that? How did I get in here? I remember staring at her, slurring my words as I tried to impress her with riveting stories to make me sound younger than I am, wondering if I'll ever get to see her naked, when... I dunno. Something silky under my feet.

And then, something else hits me.

I look at the floor. Not next to the bed, but over by the entrance to the bathroom where I see it, a pool of blood and chunks of God knows what else, formed into a little puddle of red on the tile. I throw the sheets back to stand up and realize I am in a bathrobe, not my suit from last night, and I'm completely covered in blood, possibly even someone else's. My guts hurt. I feel like I've been stabbed in the abdomen, not to mention my aching head, and my mouth is cotton dry and aching for thirst. I stand, woozily, and draw back the robe to find my torso is indeed intact, however, it's completely covered with some sort of sticky maroon slime.

Arched and twisted, I hobble toward the bathroom to inspect. I have a hard time walking, legs jacked apart like I've been riding bareback for weeks, and I falter as I enter, narrowly catching myself on the door frame when I look in.

The blood-dripped trail leads directly to the toilet which looks like the kill room of a slaughterhouse. I ease my way in, tiptoeing step by step, covering my nose due to the horrific odor emanating from the commode. The lid is covered in fingerprints, my own, perhaps? Or the victims, struggling to get away, quite possibly grabbing the only appliance in sight with which to hold? The rest of the story is clear. The walls, toilet, and the floor definitely got it the worst. It looks like the toilet overflowed its mutilated remains, dumping the bloody excretion all over the cold tile floor, where it seeped into the gray porous grout, never to be scrubbed completely clean again.

I wipe my mouth in horror, the smell alone is excruciating, so strong I can actually taste it as I try to discern who, or what, may have been slaughtered here, and how complicit, exactly, was my involvement. With hand clenched over mouth, the impending smell only intensifies, and I pull my hand away, revealing even more blood smeared across my wrist.

What have I done?

I turn to face the mirror all at once, ready to face the victim or the perpetrator, which one I am still unsure, when I see it—the bloody goop across my chest and down my legs and seeped into the fabric of the white cotton robe and draped over the toilet bowl like a volcanic

explosion of blood and guts, all coagulated into dark brown puddles all over the room, each and every one of which originated from one singular logical place.

My mouth.

"My God," I say aloud as my head rings in agony.

I can taste my own death.

So many questions fill my head. Was she here? Did she see me, retching my guts out all over the pee-stained commode? Did she dress me? Or undress me? Where is my suit? What did I say? When did this happen? Is that blood, or just those red drinks we were drinking? I'm pretty sure it's both, judging from the scratch in my throat and decide there's only one thing in the world for me to do right this very second: Get in the shower and wash this shit off. The smell alone is about to make me hurl all over again.

The scalding water against the back of my head feels great. Hot. Steamy. I wash the puke off myself and flatten my cheek against the cold marble wall. That combination of blistering hot skin against freezing cold tile is just the ticket. I wake up to a lukewarm water-boarding from the spigot above as I lie spread eagle on the warm marble floor with a septum splitting headache. Probably from getting so God damn drunk yesterday. Or it could have something to do with this knot on the back of my head and the fact that I'm sprawled out on the shower floor. At least the sand's off my feet and nobody's actually dead. Both are a huge relief. I step out of the shower and directly into an invisible pile of grit. Futile, I think, as I towel off and get dressed.

I decide to go casual today. Not because my suit's lying in a puddle of bile on the hotel room floor, it wasn't the right suit anyway, but because… I dunno… I just do. I'm feeling whimsical today, something I haven't felt in a long time. Something completely contradictory to the horrific crime scene I left in the bathroom for the maid to have to deal with. I leave an extra twenty on the bed stand today, in addition to the one I usually leave. This place should be immaculate when I get back.

The buffet's not as crowded today. I figure it must be closing time again until I get to the egg station where an attendant asks me how I'd like mine cooked. I say medium rare for my own amusement. His

scowl tells me we don't share the same sense of humor. Tourists keep filtering in, selecting tables and chairs amongst the salespeople who are already seated, clacking away with the super-fans, who are face painted and ready to go.

It must be early, I consider. I wouldn't know. I lost track of my phone at the airport and I haven't seen it since. My entire life is on that phone. Emails. Contacts. People I never call, but should. Apps I downloaded, but never use. Bookmarked news articles I've never read and probably never will. Usually I'd care about these things, no, usually I would be frantically, *maniacally* tossing the house, the hotel, the car, the wherever I think it might be, in order to recover the thing seconds after it left my sight, but I'm on vacation, sort of, and I don't have anyone trying to get in touch with me but my Manager and my Mother, and quite frankly, they could be the same person. Funny how you seek out the same traits in people you surround yourself with later in life that you grew up with because those are the types of people that you identify with and already feel comfortable around. There are a lot of terms for that, but I think the one that rings most true for me is Stockholm Syndrome.

With time to kill I consider my options. There's the assignment, of course. The ball game. Not looking forward to facing that again. Those crowds. That chaos. That treacherous coliseum that could be taken down at any second by agitated North Vietnamese bombers looking to reenact their version of Pearl Harbor, or worse, rioting super-fans, either inconsolably angry or incomprehensibly hyperactive after the loss, or win, of a big tournament game. I stare at these mongrels with utter contempt; face painted, lettered, numbered, and colorfully checkering the room. There's no way in hell I'm dealing with that again. Not today. Even though some of these pricks probably drank more than me yesterday, if that's even possible, here they are, cheery and dressed up in their uniforms and war paint and they're rearing to go. And here I am, adding a seventh shot of espresso to my sugar and milk with the hopes of reviving internal organs I may have accidentally killed off in the middle of the night.

So I sit, immobilized except for my thoughts and the ability to stir. The song of the metal spoon against the chiming porcelain mug

grounds me to my seat and like a petal from the tree of knowledge, I blossom to a new awareness: It is only because of the assignment that I am afforded this luxury, this trip, this coffee, these eggs, these servants. Without it, I have nothing, and because of it, everything. If I want more assignments it behooves me to stay focused, stay the course, and continue down the beaten path. But then, as I sip from my chipped and faded mug, I think of the orange leather ball, bouncing up and down, constantly being dribbled, rattling across the basketball court in my brain as it smacks against the hardwood cerebellum and vibrates around my skull. There is no way I can sit through another agonizing exposition in a repeat of yesterday. I'd rather be dribbled, tossed, passed and dunked into the tiny metal hoop myself. And instantaneously my spectrum of options for the day becomes infinitely wider and my spirits collectively brighten.

I could go to the sales meeting. Check out the bimbos with the fake boobs, big hair, and veneer smiles, or antagonize the barrel-chested fast-talkers who like to argue about the potential for catastrophic fluctuations in the marketplace based on corruption, politics, and fickle consumers. I could hang out with all the hotheads and dickheads, coke heads, and big spenders overcompensating for their little weiners, but just thinking about all the cologne and perfume and hair gel and hair spray and close-talking and hand talking and mouth breathing and cigarette breath and wine-stained teeth and spittle and hot mouths and armpit odor and every other gross human secretion up in my face and up my nose and in my mouth and it literally makes my stomach churn, and before I know it I'm choking down the last of my coffee on the verge of vomiting it all right back out again.

I hadn't thought of her for nearly forty-five minutes when she slowly crept back into my brain. Somewhere between the headaches and the queasy stomach and the lilting disdain for the people I surround myself with a quiet little bubble burst, warming up everything around me, everything inside me, and I wonder where she is. What she's doing. How I can get in touch with her.

I flag down the waitress, who I'm fairly positive thinks I'm insane.

"Excuse me, have you seen Mena?"

"I, uh…"

She looks uncertain, as if I'm speaking a tribal language foreign to her.

"Mena? The girl that works at the tiki bar?"

"She doesn't get here 'til 6."

"Yeah, I know. Do you know where I can find her?"

"I uh… I'm sorry, sir. I can't tell you that."

She scurries away and I watch as she whispers something to her manager, a burly black guy, and someone I am not eager to meet on more personal grounds. He bites his lip and stares at me as he listens, which I feel confident is not a sign of politeness, so I quickly flag down my waiter, sign for my rubbery overcooked eggs, and leave.

The buses are lining up outside again, only these aren't your typical mega bus liners that usually prowl around the island, they're smaller ones. Like chubby gray short buses holding maybe thirty people apiece, lined up like boxcars in a long train around the resort's circle drive, completely blocking the valet station and the sole taxi available for a lift. I glance around at all the tourists milling aimlessly about, heads in their brochures, in their phones, and under their hats. What's with all these hats? Is it supposed to rain? I look up to find one lonely, wispy cloud in the pastel blue sky, hardly the kind of cloud that summons rain. These people look interesting to me. They aren't your typical tourists. They know something I don't know. Even so, I hop in the taxi to escape their growing encroachment and sigh with relief.

The driver, a jolly fellow with a red round face, gleams at me from the front seat.

"Aloha!"

"Aloha."

"Where to?"

"Surprise me."

I can feel my pulse quicken as the words escape my lips.

Now I'm in for it. A real adventure. The embarking of a new journey, destination unknown. A train off the rails, but with an engineer in full control, and a lot of cash. I'll have to pay it back, of course, unless I can come up with a good excuse for why it's gone, but I'm not worried about that now. Let's get this adventure started already.

"Excuse me?" he asks, voice full of trepidation. Confusion.

"Surprise me," I clarify. "Take me someplace cool. Someplace, I dunno... exotic. Maybe somewhere tourists don't usually go."

He stares out the front window, presumably at the hat-headed tourists milling about in front of his taxi, slowly boarding the short buses that pin him in. I can hear the wheels turning in his head, not from the rusty grind of metal teeth forcefully grating between the gears, but the audible moan he releases between his agape lips as he stares emotionless into his future. Here we are, in Paradise, an island in the middle of nowhere, with a volcano you can hike, turtles you can swim with, world-class resorts, helicopter tours to nearby islands to see lost civilizations of lepers... There are literally endless things to do.

And my driver can't think of one.

What does it matter? We're trapped anyway. I can't go anywhere until these buses move. Might as well wait for him to come up with something good. Something *great* even, if we sit here long enough.

Aquariums. Surfing haunts. Great local restaurants. Beautiful lookouts. Fishing coves. Paddle-board rentals. Kite surfing, maybe.

Finally, an idea springs into his jelly head. "Oh, I know..." And he looks at me with great fervor. "I've got just the thing. Very special this time of year. Most people don't know about it, but if you're from the mainland, you'll like it very much."

I nod, eagerly. Now, this is what I'm talking about. Excitement. A journey. *Adventure.* Just what I always wanted.

"You like college basketball?"

The taxi door slams behind me as I pace into the crowd, and without warning, without second thought, as if I'd planned it subconsciously all along but lacked the cojones to act out on the rawest of impulses, I casually step onboard one of the short buses and move swiftly down the aisle, taking a seat in the back beside an older fellow in a loud floral shirt halfway into his nap. Before I know it everyone's aboard, a whole bus full of people in hats, which they take off upon sitting, leaving one man awkwardly remaining up front, searching the bus for a seat that's not there. He yanks off his hat and looks everyone over, skimming the tops of our heads with a stern look, as if to guilt the

guilty into self-persecution, into admitting their wrongdoings and seat stealing so they can be forcibly ejected so that he can take his rightful place on this borrowed seat of a mildew-infested, stiflingly hot short bus, hat and all. Only I don't give in. I ignore him. And just as quickly as he stepped on, his mask of optimism blurs into a sad plea of thanksgiving and the bus driver shakes his head. The guy slaps his cap back over his forehead and the overflow boils from the vessel like bubbles from a test tube, dribbling down the stairs and away from the bus in a disenchanted acceptance that this is his life now, however new and estranged, and this tour, or whatever this is, and wherever we are going, is no longer for him. I watch him through the dark tinted glass of the picture window as he follows the line of tourists around the circle driveway and disappears onto a different bus. I mean, I guess he got on another bus, I can't really see from here, all the other buses are in the way. Maybe we're all going the same place. Or maybe not. I don't know where any of us are going. I have no idea who these people are, or what we're up to, or who got them together to coordinate all the hats. I know absolutely nothing. But at this point, it doesn't really matter to me. Nothing really matters to me, now that I've met Mena.

It takes a little over an hour, just as we round another endless bend, sugar cane thick on either side of us, and a volcanic mountain looming up ahead, that I muster up the courage to lean over the aisle to the lady opposite me and ask,

"Where are we going again?"

She smiles, sugary sweet, like a grandmother I've known my whole life, her apple pie heart opening up to me, warming me into a puddle of vanilla ice cream by her side as she indicates her brochure.

THE ROAD TO HANA
&
THE SEVEN SACRED POOLS OF OHE'O

This means nothing to me. Who, or what is Hana? And what's the deal with these seven sacred pools? One wasn't enough? Is this some kind of spiritual enlightenment shit? What have I gotten myself into? There's a waterfall on the cover. Big freaking deal. I've seen

40

waterfalls before. There was one not too far from where I grew up. We called it a waterfall, anyway. It was dry most of the year, but it could be pretty cool when it rained. Up in the hills somewhere, where we used to explore when we were kids. It's been a while.

I smile and nod to grandma and sit back in my seat. Guess I'll just have to wait to find out what this adventure's all about. I can only hope it's not some guru shit. I close my eyes to go to sleep, joining the rest of the geriatrics along for the ride whose heads keep bobbling from side to side as we weave through the sugar cane. The view isn't much. Like a cornfield of leafy stalks, blowing in the wild Hawaiian wind. It doesn't take much to sway me to sleep.

I awaken in the old man's lap, my stomach churning. He's bickering at me to get off him, but he's the one that's been slobbering all over me, sleeping with his head on my shoulder since we left, the crazy bastard. He's missing a bottom tooth, so as he yammers on about the entitlement issues of the youth he spits soured bile all over my shirt. I try to ignore it out of respect, but it's difficult, and I find myself wiping the spittle from my eyelid more than once. Despite my complete agreement with his dissertation, I fail to understand the correlation between his vitriolic diatribe and me. *I'm* not the youth to which he refers. He could be my dad. Kind of looks like him even, with a lot less hair. Course, once you get to that age and you're demoted to wearing corduroy pants and argyle sweaters every day everybody kinda looks the same. Especially the hair, or what's left of it. There's no wonder why most of us evolve into bitter entitled assholes as we age. We start off so innocent and sweet, taught to be open-minded and polite, and Jesus Loves Us and Somewhere Over the Rainbow and The Sun'll Come Out Tomorrow and all that other bullshit, but over time the empty chalkboard of life gets scribbled on and sun-damaged and scratched up and covered in paint and the frame gets chipped and broken, and before you know it the damn thing's left dangling from the nail you strung it from years before until eventually it falls and the masterpiece you've been working on your whole life comes tumbling down on top of you. And after putting up with everyone else's shit for your entire life, you finally get a chance to speak your mind and act for

41

yourself when somebody else comes along and puts you back in diapers.

The bus wheels right and everyone sways left. I'm in his lap again, and he's scowling at me when we flip, the bus wheels left and he comes barreling over me, apologizing profusely as he grabs for something to pull him off. He's still apologizing, trying to hold on to the bar in the back of the seat ahead of him when I go flying into his seat and up against the window.

"If you're not already buckled, you might want to consider doing that now" comes a jolly voice from the speaker over my head. I look at that old lady opposite me and she sits contently, a soft smile across her face, calmly buckled in her seat. Her shoulders sway evenly with the rhythm of the turning bus, back and forth, back and forth, baaaaack…

I'm searching for my seat belt when I'm tossed into her lap, only she's not smiling anymore. I thrust myself back into the hard, concave seat where my bony ass grinds against the plywood seat bottom. "Cheap piece of shit," I mutter, as the old lady continues to frown at me. I grab the wildly swinging strap at my side and buckle it into the holster when suddenly I'm in the old timer's lap all over again.

"Tighten the hatches," he says, indicating the nub of fabric I can pull to tighten the seat belt that's apparently been lengthened to max capacity to accommodate the eight-hundred-pound orca that must have been strapped down here before me.

"Jesus H."

I finally get my hatches tightened, yet I continue to sway from the waist up, like the old lady beside me, into and out of the aisle with my geriatric dancing partners on either side and all around. It's like a Busby Berkeley musical and I'm Buster Keaton. The old-timer smiles at me, laughing practically. He must be watching the same film. Or maybe he knows I have this raging headache, and these dramatic turns keep shaking up all the coffee in my stomach and he's mocking me. Hell, this is practically a rollercoaster ride in his book. He's probably having a blast. The lady on the other side resumes her Buddhist calm, holding steadfast to the seat in front of her, barely swaying an inch

when suddenly I see it. The whole bus sees it, or maybe they knew it was there the whole time.

Out our picture window, the view is breathtaking. Our visibility is infinite in every direction, up into the pale sunlit sky or out across the deep blue sea, both meeting on the distant horizon where the power harnessed by two completely different worlds collide into a perfect and infinite seam.

But below, there are three hundred-foot cliffs straight down, leading to a rocky bed of boulders that have fallen from above, where the mighty ocean meets the soil in an explosive collision between relentless surging energies. It's breathtaking yet horrifying. But as hard as the ocean beats against the rock walls below, the cliffs hold strong, holding granite beds and tree trunks and grassy knolls and lava-like asphalt, asphalt which has been poured over Paradise in a serpentine outline of the island as a dangerous boundary not to be crossed.

We aren't just swerving inside this death trap of a bus for no reason, right? Surely we're carving out 180-degree switchbacks around the cliff-lined coast toward these seven sacred pools because they're guaranteed to be life-altering, no? I mean, there's no other reason for this. Whatever it is, the payoff must be extraordinary.

Maybe we're going to the Fountain of Youth! Judging from the cocoon of octogenarians on this bus I think that's quite likely. All of us shuttling together toward hallowed ground so mystical that there is but one way to get there, by cheating death. With little more than a tree, or a shrub, or a boulder, and a scraped-up guard rail, or sometimes nothing but the gravel which is slowly cracking off the edge of the pavement beside us, falling to the endless body of saltwater below like a Road Runner cartoon, we travel along this frightening Road to Hana, scared out of our minds. There is no median. There is no place to pull off. Around some turns there aren't even two lanes, or room for more than a Fiat, much less a mildewed luxury shortbus such as this to pass through. We're facing inescapable death, and there's absolutely nothing we can do about it.

I can't help but wonder if any of this is in that brochure with the waterfalls grandma's holding about the sacred swimming pools and whatnot. By now my stomach is swelling inside me, pushing all of my

43

internal organs up into my chest, and my head is pounding to the internal beat of a silent drum, so I try to pick a spot on the horizon to hold my attention, and hopefully, keep my headache at bay. But the bus turns so rapidly around a never-ending stream of elastic switchbacks that an ocean of bile slowly rises in my stomach, roaring through me like a tidal wave of fuel before it crashes against the rock lining of my gut.

"Breathtaking, huh?" The old-timer questions, as if I need convincing. I try to focus the best I can on the blurred line where the sky meets the water. My head swims, and as the bus sways around continued curves, my eyes slowly lull into submission until at last, I'm asleep.

I wake up with my head against the window. The bus has stopped. The old timer's sitting in my seat, arms folded, bottom lip pursed. I have no idea how we switched seats.

Then, the old-timer files off the bus with the rest of them, as in the people who actually paid money for this trip, and I try to maintain a level of composure, afraid that any sudden movement might stimulate an evacuation of contents, so I sit. I can't really see shit from back here, because of a big tree in my way but there's some kind of an old wooden sign that I can't quite make out. I can only assume that this is it. This is the big reveal. This is what we all came for. And despite my current dilemma, I'm ready to see what it's all about. I peel my hair off the glass and stand up, woozily. After three espresso laden cups of coffee, I'm far from drunk, but this Road to Hana shit is making me dizzy.

I get out of the bus to find myself in a gravel parking lot. This is not exciting. Some suicidal bus driver is trying to kill us, and for what? A gravel lot? I could have gone to Albuquerque for this. Where am I and what am I doing here, that's all I want to know. I should have stayed in the sandy bed this morning, at least it was warm. Or maybe in the shower, where I could have choked on my own vomit when I threw up and then at very least I wouldn't still have to turn in three pages about some trivial game I'm not even attending. I wonder what the score is. Here or there. I check my pockets for my phone. It's lost, I remember. I haven't seen it since the taxi stand, back at the airport, when I called to complain about the disorganization of drink service on

the flight. I have no idea what time it is, but the air still has that early morning chill. I wait for a moment, momentarily paralyzed by the swaying inside my brain, and I watch the traffic in the parking lot like it's a Godfrey Reggio film. Like clockwork, for every car that pulls in, another one pulls out in a synchronized exchange of vehicles as they appear and disappear in a continuous loop around the lot. And every car that pulls in seems to unload a healthy-looking bunch of explorers, all of whom depart eagerly from their vehicles with their cameras and water bottles and cell phones and start hiking up.

Up? Up to where? Is this for real right now? I just rode in the serpent's belly for over an hour and a half at least just so I could stand in a gravel pit of a parking lot and hike *up*?

Oh… what the fuck. I've got nothing better to do. Besides, I'm here, and it seems pretty peaceful. A city man could use some peace every now and then. Especially when he's in Paradise.

And like that, I put one flip-flopped foot in front of the other and I hike. There's a cool breeze on my toes. This is nicer than I remember. My thighs burn under the intense pressure of my out of shape body weight, and I sweat. I can hear the brook not far off, and some Hawaiian rednecks, who even knew there was such a thing, blasting some awful bullshit they call music, which makes me hike all the faster to get past them and on up the mountain. One of them has his shirt off. He really shouldn't. Why do rednecks always have to take their shirt off?

Ten minutes later I have to take my shirt off. It's so fucking hot I can hardly stand it. I haven't sweated this much in, well, ever. I mean, for late November, this is crazy. Or maybe it's my body heat, boiling over from the intense amount of strain and pressure I'm steadily applying to my overworked and slightly fatty heart-shaped box. Worse, I keep smelling an awful repugnant smell over and over again like it's following me. Or maybe it's my breath. Either way, it's awful. I don't even care anymore. I just keep going. Onward and upward until I reach the top. The summit. The place that this bus and twelve identical buses from all over the island have descended. This place called Hana, wherever it is, at the top of this mountain. Or trail. Or wherever I'm going. Whatever I'm doing.

I pass an older couple on the way down and they certainly look at peace. Like they've been to the peak of the mountaintop, and they've seen all there is to see. Maybe I shouldn't be so judgmental of people, I consider. I'm on vacation, or, I guess *now* I'm on vacation, now that I've thrown caution to the wind, as well as judgment and the assignment, and my day, and everything else I know on this island, so what do I care if those guys back there don't have any shirts on? I look at my pasty white arms with disgust. They look like fatty PVC pipes. Like hairy, lilting cylinders draped between bony shoulders and wrists. I could use a tan, I think. I wonder how long that takes?

Within ten minutes my skin is flecked with cancerous sunspots. It burns just to touch it. I'm forced to put my shirt on, and I'm panting like a bloodhound. I pause on the trail as I gasp for breath when suddenly, through a gap in the trees, I see it...

Paradise.

Or mini-paradise, perhaps. Past the thick of the woods, down a narrow beaten path, there's a clearing. And in the clearing lies a crystal-clear pool with a sandy white basin and solid gray boulders plunked around to form the rim of nature's swimming hole. A worn but sturdy fallen tree serves as a bridge to cross over the small brook if you don't want to hop any more boulders and when I step up on it I look up to see the sprinkle of the waterfall as it splashes into a pool from the rock ledge twelve feet above. The pool trickles through the rocks beneath the tree bridge to form a luminous stream down the hill. I can hardly believe my eyes as I pause to admire it.

This is a waterfall. Maybe not, like, what I imagined the Fountain of Youth to look like, but it's at least as good as something from of a Thomas Kinkade painting. Maybe better since it's real.

"Go on, friend."

I turn to see the redneck with no shirt and wonder what's his hurry.

"Sorry," I reply.

I step off the other end of the log to give them room and I put my shirt back on. I take a minute for myself, to admire the serenity of this lush, mysterious, yet vibrant planet we live on, when suddenly, as if a timer has gone off, an invisible dam breaks and a sea of hats pours

out from the pool above and down the dirt path heading straight for me. I close my eyes as if I can make them go away, when I feel the hairy arms of men and tangled purses of women as they rush past me, scraping against my body, pulling me along, and then I look up, and I'm being carried in the wave of geriatric hats as they storm the ground home. I fight against it, kicking and flailing so as not to lose my stake on this heavenly pond, but after crossing the tree bridge and stumbling over a rocky stream I come to realize that like it or not, my bus is leaving. And I really don't want to be left here. I feel a wave of relief wash over me. That might not have been the Fountain of Youth I wanted it to be, but at last, I surmise, we're finally going home.

*   *   *   *   *

The bus grinds to a halt around every turn, then jolts forward again for no more than an eighth of a mile at a time, over and over like some sort of lurching rollercoaster, not offering the heights and plunges of your typical amusement park ride so much as blind 180 degree turns enclosed by rocky cliffs on one side and an endless abyss on the other that swivel your eyes inside your head like cherries on a slot machine. And we're not going home. We're headed onward. We've got seven more stops, grandma eventually tells me. The last one is in Ohio, which seems a bit odd. I guess there's one out here, too.

And we're passing people in this thing. Going forty miles an hour down a one-lane road into oncoming traffic around what looks like another white-knuckled tourist hunched over the wheel of his Chevy Aveo rental as his wife screams obscenities beside him. But nobody's turning back. We just continue on our winding snake track along the coast of doom, and every thirty to forty-five minutes we pull over to inspect some further hidden trail revealing a whole new Paradise of trails and trail seekers, waters and falls, foliage and nature, and then we're off again. The road folds back on itself like the years of my life, retreading the same old ground over and over while the passengers keep searching around the next bend for that straightaway that will carry us forward without rolling back again. The proverbial two steps forward, one step back, as demonstrated via a windy asphalt

47

road with no room for error on either side, as we constantly pursue forward directions to reach our unknown destination beyond the mountain.

The ride itself becomes a tantric blur as we sway in unison around the turns, a wondrous display of synchronized sitting, as each and every passenger on the bus tries to hold ourselves in place as best we can lest we pop all over the cheaply upholstered mildew stained seats. As we collectively fight to squelch this instinctual reaction to cheating death, gravity, and digestion, we attempt to focus on the beautiful ocean or a rugged house tucked away in a thicket of trees, or a lush green pasture sprawling across an open hill. We swerve atop the criminally dangerous cliffs with mortifying intentions, with a bus driver seemingly intent on riding in the lane nearest the edge, when there is, in fact, such a lane, even though that lane is clearly reserved for oncoming traffic heading back west, back toward the resorts and the airports, back toward the sugar cane fields and civilization, and as far away from this mysterious destination Hana as they can get.

I still have no idea what the point to all of this is, but we obviously haven't found it, as we refuse to turn around. I hold the bile at bay in the nether regions of my throat for as long as humanly possible until we unload into another gravel lot and I charge to the front, spewing into the nearest barrel trash can or available bush. And then we hike. Upwards and onwards, where we are sure to discover yet another charming natural spring, with a cool clear pond inviting us to swim, and the warm beating sun that shafts through feathered leaves above onto my warm skin where it strikes an unfamiliar glow upon my face. The calming sound of a long urination trickles eternally from the waterfall over the ridge into the basin of the swimming hole below. Each place we stop is more incredible than the last. Each has its own unique landscape. Its own way of adapting to the elements. Its own identity.

But after three of four Gardens of Eden, they all start to taste the same. Even with all of this beauty surrounding us, I can hardly take it anymore. Not the waterfalls. Not Paradise. And definitely not that short bus ride on the Road to Hell, or Hana, whichever stop we get to first. I don't even care what's on the other side of it. I don't care if it's the Tree

of Life itself and for twenty extra bucks you get to pick the fruit. I don't care about anything, I'm just ready for this serpentine nightmare to be over.

Besides, I'm thinking about her again and six o'clock can't get here fast enough. Is it six o'clock yet? Who here might know? I'm standing in the middle of God knows where Maui Wowwi and the sun is blazing hot, and I've got no way to get back to the hotel except for the death trap of a short bus, and my feet are fucking killing me and I don't have a clue where I am. I realize I'm getting over-agitated, and when I get over-agitated I need to sit down, so I do. Right on a cool, wet boulder along a narrow ledge beside the swimming hole. It's large enough to lie back on, so I do, and it feels good to rest like this, despite the hard granite bed I've chosen, and as I look up I'm surprised to find the tiniest beam of sunlight streaming directly into my eyes. A single ray of light penetrates the leafy canopy above to blind me and within seconds I see spots. I close my eyes and everything spins like I'm still on that bus. I feel like I'm blacking out only I'm completely awake. I open my eyes again to make it stop, but I'm forced to close them again, giving in to the notions of retinal pain, spotty vision, and exhaustion, which is when I notice something I only partially realized before: someone here is smoking pot.

I sit up abruptly and immediately spot them. A motley looking trio of dudes half my age strolling up the hill to the top of the falls. They weren't on the bus. They're not tourists. They're probably in that raggedy old VW bus I saw pulling into the lot just about the time I finished yacking in the barrel trash can at the base of the hill. I wasn't even sick this morning when I left, despite what the bathroom looked like. If it weren't for that damned bus ride I bet I wouldn't be hungover at all. And those eggs. Those eggs were disgusting. I should have never gagged those down.

But that pot will make me feel better. Pot will subdue the pain in my brain and the spinning inside. Pot will make that awful taste in my mouth go away, replaced by a new and different awful taste, one that will make this entire joyride a little more joyful.

I shuffle off my granite perch and consider my play as I wander toward the skunky aroma clouding up the woods. I pass the old-timer,

who looks at me with disgust, and a few other tourists who casually linger, ogling everyone crossways as they try to figure out the source of the fragrant smell. One lady recognizes it and inhales deeply, a wide grin across her face as she tries to cop a flashback to a simpler time. Nobody's noticed the local kids tucked away up above the falls, off the beaten path amidst the trees, on their own road toward discovery it appears. They try to be discreet in their efforts, but the lingering odor of their bubblegum kush betrays them. I've smelled some dank in my time, but this is some strong stuff right here. If I can score just a bit, maybe tomorrow I'll get high and head to the beach. I can't think of a better way to relax than that.

I used to smoke marijuana. More than a little. But I quit a while ago when I started getting serious about my life and my work. It made perfect sense at the time. Now I'm wondering what the fuck I was thinking. It smells delicious, aside from the obvious skunk aroma. Odiferous some might say. But this one smells like strawberries. I wander up the hill, lingering just outside their conversation when I hear something about some kind of golden crap or something like that, and if the field doesn't work there's a ranch nearby. Then there's something about a fence and a shotgun or something when I suddenly realize I'm getting dangerously close. Unable to contain myself any further, I unbutton the second button of my button-down shirt, grow a pair of nuts the size of Molokai and plop down on a log next to them.

"How you fella's doing?"

They look at me. Then at one another. Then back at me. This isn't good.

"You having a good afternoon?"

They look at one another again, then back at me. Still not good.

"You guys wouldn't happen to, uh, you know… have any more of that stuff you're smoking, would'ja?"

They glare at me. Then at one another. Then back at me.

Can they hear me? What the fuck is wrong with these people? Are they *that* high?

There's the nice-looking one with a backpack that looks like he just got out of school, a shaggy looking hipster who probably plays guitar in a band, and a total stoner, with wild and crazy hair, who's no

doubt lost a few marbles along the way. If they actually were a band, that guy would definitely be the drummer.

They all begin to laugh. Not some hysterical hyena-like howl of baboons, but in a casual who-the-fuck-is-this-guy, north-shore-surfer-brah, I-hope-he's-got-cash-on-him-cause-this-ain't-gonna-be-cheap endearing type of thing.

"Hahahaha. Of course, brah." The nice-looking one gives me a hard once-over, then smiles. "You wouldn't happen to have some cash on you, would you?"

Nailed it.

I open my wallet. Five hundred dollar bills. All crisp. Holographic. Fake looking they're so new. I pull out a hundred and put my wallet away.

"Whoa, dude."

I've upset them by being so forward, I can tell.

"It's cool," their head honcho says as he signals with his hands to keep it. The others snicker at him, or me, I can't tell. I fold the hundred into my pocket and try to smile. My breath stinks, I know it. These potheads don't know. They don't know shit. What the fuck are they doing all the way out here anyway? Surely they didn't drive all the way out here just to get high. Hopefully, they didn't drive at all. And maybe more importantly, how do they plan on getting back? Do people actually *live* out here?

They pass a small, purple glass pipe my way, the bowl packed to the brim with fresh skunky crystal laden buds, and I sit down beside them, one of the gang, and light only a quarter of the greens on top, remembering proper pot etiquette from my glory days. I let go of the carb and gently inhale from the long tube, where I get fruit notes immediately. Passion fruit. Mango. Mmmm. Maybe Lemon? Very refreshing. With a nice smooth finish and smoky aftertaste. I would love another, but proper etiquette demands I pass it to the scruffy looking guy beside me.

"Delicious," I offer, and for that moment and the next several moments after, I completely forget all about my headache, my stomach ache, and anything else that ever bothered me, ever.

"You know, I've tasted some bud in my time, but that... that right there... is amazing."

They accept the compliment with gleaming faces.

"Duper grows it," announces the weird-looking guy with long crazy hair.

I look at him like a Cocker Spaniel, floppy ears and all. Was that even English?

"I'm sorry, did you just say *Duper*?"

The poor schmuck who obviously answers to this name grins with charming modesty. "Yeah." It's the same guy that packed the bowl. The nice-looking guy. You've got to be kidding me.

The scruffy guy skips a turn, handing the bowl across to the drummer, who MacGyver's the lighter into a flame-throwing fire hazard, puts his lips gently against the swirled purple tube and blazes the remaining weed in the bowl into ashy oblivion. I guess chivalry amongst potheads is dead, too. He cashes out the entire bowl, then hands it back to Duper, who packs another bowl without even being asked.

I examine the dopey bastard with pity. "How'd you get a name like that?"

"Just lucky I guess."

Duper passes the bowl to his other friend, Chris, the scruffy kid with dirty feet who waves it off again, before taking the hit himself. He lights the corner, just like I did, but maybe a little more, and inhales deeply. He looks at me, and on seeing my eager anticipation, hands me the bowl. I take it and am happy to see there is still a little bit of green showing on top. It's not all burnt and ashy. The bowl is half full. Maybe this is a turning point for me and my adventure. Maybe I'll find Paradise after all. And as I'm thinking all of this I realize Duper hasn't even exhaled yet. I put the lighter to the bowl and inhale when I quickly realize that I'm the one that's being duped; there might have appeared to be a shiny plot of grass in the bowl, but underneath was all barren and dry. I cough and spew clumps of burnt ash from my mouth as Duper slowly exhales.

"Sorry 'bout that, brah." I hand the pipe back across to him, hoping he will refill it as casually as he did before and hand it back to

me, as we potheads break bread with one another, smoking from a pipe of peace like his ancestors before him, but he sticks it in his deep cargo pocket and everyone stands.

I look over the edge of the waterfall, hoping that my knees don't cave in beneath me on these swollen rotting feet, admiring the view through the trees, and the bird's eye view of the pond below, and the tourists and the adventurers and everyone else that has traveled this day just to come and be here and see this. And suddenly I realize… the hat-headed old-timers, the Japanese camera crew, the Tommy Bahama/Lilly Pulitzer set and all the other Tourists that filled up the short buses on the way here are now gone, replaced by a whole new crop of imbeciles wading up to the pool of tranquility from the trail below with wondrous gasps and whispers.

"It's magnificent." I overhear one of the newcomers say.

"Amazing," another concurs.

"Fucking great…" I add, presumably in my head.

Duper's friends suddenly charge off purposefully into the woods, the opposite direction from the trail. I look at Duper, almost certainly full of fear and confusion, but it's muddled by the thick cloud of smoke that lingers between us.

"You okay?"

"I think I missed my bus."

Duper waves his arm through the air like it's of little to no concern. And maybe it's not, for him. But for me that ride back is everything. As bad as it was, at least it gets me out of here, wherever here is, exactly.

"Follow me."

I look into his bloodshot eyes, questioning his intentions, and I'm still trying to get my sea legs back from my lifelong hiatus from working out, but I'm high as a kite and he looks sincere and I'm eager to see where this adventure leads, so sure, what the hell.

Urgency, if you can call it that, bubbles inside him as his friends leave him behind. "C'mon. We got a long way to go if we're gonna make it in time."

Normally this kind of vagueness would preclude me from attempting to follow along with such haste, but here, now, it seems

perfectly sensible, and I trudge excitedly along behind them into the unknown, already heaving for breath in the hot midday sun as we keep pushing farther and farther away from the tourist beaten path.

Within a few minutes I can't help but ask.

"Umm... Where is it that we're going?"

"You wanna see something cool?"

I hate it when people answer a question with a question. Of course I want to see something cool, that's the only reason anybody ever does anything, right? But that doesn't answer my question as to where it is, exactly, that we are going to see this cool thing because right now we are headed in the exact opposite direction from the gravel parking lot below that leads us home. I follow behind as closely as I can, as Duper whips between branches and rocks and jumps over streams and fallen logs in his way.

What am I doing? I'm following them into certain death, I'm sure. I've seen this movie before, where they lead me deep into the woods until finally they attack me and hogtie me to a post and chant at me before burning me alive, all in the name of some sacred religious right protected by the IRS. Yet I travel onward, gasping for air, just beyond their last man, Duper, at all times. Through the woods. Through the trees. Into some abandoned field where we pause for an inordinate amount of time to examine large clods of dirt before we continue onward. Over the brook. And down the hill.

For a bunch of potheads, they're swift little buggers. My shirt's wide open now, like the mainsail of a ship, or a kite hanging in the wind, which happens to feel great but also keeps me caught in the breeze, just far enough behind that I lose sight of them every once in a while, only to catch up to them a few minutes later in the unlikeliest of places... The parking lot. I land in the hard gravel like a fish out of water, sopping wet and gasping for breath.

"Pretty cool, huh?" Duper stands with the others, lighting cigarettes.

"It's a short cut." Chris clarifies.

And sure enough, they're right. There's my bus. And there's the old-timer getting on as we speak. There are a half dozen other buses that look the exact same. Another old fart gets on a different bus. It's

like some sort of alternate universe happening right beside itself. These people all look the same.

"Whoa." I'm tripping out, there's really no question. Duper turns to me, concerned.

"You okay, man?"

"Yeah, I'm good."

"You miss your bus?"

"No. I don't think so. Not yet."

"Oh, cool. Well... Good luck." We shake. He tries something complicated and it immediately falls into awkward fist-bumping.

"Yeah man. Thanks. You, too. And thanks for helping me get back."

"No worries, bro."

And as they head to their car across the parking lot the words spill out of my mouth before I even know what I'm saying. "Hey, is there, uh... Any way you guys have room for one more?"

Duper searches me, curiously.

"I uh... I got so sick on that bus... I'm not sure I'll make it if I'm trapped in there again. I mean, I don't know where you're going, but if you don't mind..."

Duper turns around to his friends, who look at each other, cautiously. He turns back again and sizes me up more seriously.

"I mean... I don't want to impose."

I don't even know why I'm saying this. I don't want to ride with these people. They're serial ax murders, just waiting to get me alone in the back of their car, or in the trunk. They're high as kites, floating somewhere just below cloud nine. They're little kids who probably drive even more carelessly on this ridiculous road than our seasoned bus driver.

"No, it's just... we're not going to Ohe'o. We're only going as far as Hana."

There it is again... That *Hana*. What is this place? And what wonders does it offer?

"Oh, okay..." I try to sound less interested, although now I want it more than ever.

"We got a little business to take care of just past Lyons Hill, then we can take you as far back as Paia."

I have no idea what he's talking about, but I seize every opportunity to get anywhere but here.

"I mean, if you can fit me… I don't want to be a burden."

The guys share nervous looks between them once more.

"No, hoaloha. It's cool." Hedging his bet, "It *could* get a little crowded on the way home…" heavy emphasis on the *could*. It's obvious he doesn't want to say yes, but he's too nice to tell a stranger no… "But, if you're cool…"

He looks right at me, *into* me, examining my intentions like a suspicious mother after breaking curfew on a school night. "Are you cool, man? I mean, like, are you *cooool*?"

The way he said it was cool. I mean, comparatively, I'm definitely not as cool as he is, that's obvious. But I can't say that. Of course I'm cool. They wouldn't have shared that bowl or given me the time of day if they didn't think I was cool. I'm as cool as they come. Especially at my age.

"Yeah, man. Of course." I give him my best bro nod, which barely passes muster, before standing back on my haunches, arms crossed in the coolest *I'm so cool I don't give a fuck about nothing, not even you* pose and return his dubious glare. Hopefully, he's forgotten the bungled handshake.

"You still got that hundred on you?"

"Oh, yeah." I fish it excitedly from my pocket, then abruptly pause to consider how I'll write this off. Concessions at the games? But what about receipts? The only cash expense I'm expected to have that's covered by the stipend that I wouldn't have to account for with a receipt is a bribe for inside information or better athlete access, like behind the scenes. But I have neither. I hand the hundred over anyway. Duper doesn't even look at it, he just shoves it in his pocket.

"Alright… I guess you can tag along. Just don't tell nobody, cool?"

There's that word again. And ironically, no, it's getting hot as shit out here.

"Yea. *Cool*, man. No worries."

The weird-looking guy looks nervous, but that just might be how he looks. When I make eye contact he smiles. Chris and Duper shrug, carefree, like they've never met a stranger, and Duper opens the back door for me to get in. I glance back at the bus, which waits patiently for a tourist who'll never come, when I swear the angry gentleman whose seat I originally took sneaks back on, making things all right in the world again. I take it as a prophetic sign and hop in the tiny back seat of the car, where I wonder at which point they will chop my feet off and bind me to the roof with a hood ornament in my mouth. But whatever painful torture awaits me, it's bound to be better than riding on that God-forsaken short bus.

My head's outside the window gasping for air in no time flat. I totally should have taken the bus. I should never have smoked that weed. And I never should have come on this cursed Road to Hana, which, much to my dismay, I have finally learned is nothing more than a tiny fishing town. Not the Fountain of Youth. Not some great Mecca or Haven of Intellectuals or Celebrities, and certainly not some kind of Mystical Spiritual Guide who would have cleansed my being with his purity of thought and clarity of vision, in turn filling me with passion, drive and purpose in this life, which I am so desperately seeking. No. None of that. Instead, I hear it's a quaint, re: shitty, little town with nothing to do, nothing to visit, no place to go, and nothing to see. I mean, really? WTF, man? Is this the ultimate Hawaiian practical joke? Captivate tourists with the promise of unrivaled scenic beauty and glorious water spilling from the rocks above into the ocean, before torturing them by strapping them inside a steel death trap on the treacherous Road to Hana for hours on end. I don't remember seeing *that* in the brochure.

And abruptly, we stop. The doors pop open. They're out. They've been saying something about 'Right up here' and 'do you think he's okay' for the last couple minutes, but I'm certainly surprised to find that when I open the door I'm standing in the middle of the road. I slam the door shut to find myself on a narrow gravel shoulder when a car blares its horn as it rolls past at five miles an hour, any faster on this screwball highway would be criminal, and I casually walk to the side of the road. I see Duper following Chris as the crazy-haired

kid squeezes through a break in a ten-foot wooden fence, leading into what looks like an orchard of some kind, judging from whatever kind of trees those are. Duper waves me over, then squeezes through the fence, and by the time I get there I've lost sight of them. It's like they're purposefully trying to get rid of me. Did they just ditch their own car to do it? I mean, we are pretty high, but even I know that's stupid. No, there's something else. He mentioned something about being crowded on the way home, after running an errand. Something's going on here, and I'm due to find out what. Curiosity springs through my mind like an Olympian gymnast, so I suck in my gut and scramble to push myself through the slick rotten wood as quickly as I can so as not to be left behind.

I follow the trio past the orchard and into the woods, the only difference between the two being the sudden haphazardness and variety of the trees. We continue past a narrow brook that I can only assume at one point or another winds itself into one of those majestic waterfalls we've been hiking up to, or maybe it mists whimsically into the sea from a hundred and seventy foot drop off, like I imagine the short bus doing, with thirty passengers evaporating into thin air on the way down. Before long I tire and find myself lagging even further behind, as I am overweight and out of shape and a couple decades past my prime, as the buoyant teens speed through the trees racing toward something beyond the moss-filled woods. And then I see a clearing ahead and I charge forward, out of the shade and into a pouring hot stream of sunlight. We're in a pasture, and they whip giant trash bags from their pockets and start kicking through the grass with their shoes, the black plastic sails billowing in the wind as they appear to take flight. Occasionally, somebody will reach over and delicately pluck something thin, white, and frail from a large hunk of mud in the pasture. I watch, enchanted by their amusement when I step forward into a huge clump of hardened dirt myself.

"Shit."

I hover on one leg, with my other knee up, my sandaled foot planted firmly on the ground as another harbors a mud cake stuck to the bottom of my sole.

As Duper delicately plucks a long fragile phallus from a hardened brownie cake, I lean in, carefully scraping the mud patty off my flip flop, and immediately notice a remarkable stench arising from the pasture, as well as my foot. I kneel over to the loosened mud cake to get a proper smell and promptly gag.

"UGCKKHHHHHH!"

"Are you okay?"

I look around, despondently. I don't understand. I'm in the twilight zone, and the smell of my breath is suddenly no match for that of my feet.

"What is that... *Shit*?"

I want there to be other answers. I want him to tell me that these shit patties have nutritional value and healing properties and by stepping in one I am actually releasing neurotoxins from my body that will now make me immune to bacterial diseases and cancer. But I know better.

"Where are we?"

Duper looks around as if it couldn't be more obvious.

"Cow pasture."

This means nothing to me, and thus, I glare, contemptuously. I might not be on fire right now, or missing any hastily chopped off limbs, or tied to the hood of the car, but I just stepped into a heaping pile of cow shit because these hippies have driven me further out into the middle of nowhere and lead me into the woods where they are out collecting bovine turds for some pharmacological science project I couldn't begin to understand and I've about had enough. I'm tired. Exhausted, even. My feet are blistered, my knees ache, thighs are burning, and I'm liable to either puke again or keel over from dehydration at any given minute. And more than anything, I want it to be six o'clock. I want to go back to the resort. It's past time to tiki.

I hobble over toward a clump of long grass where I proceed to wipe the murky cow shit from my flops, and for the first time note the dozen or so bewildered cows grazing in the same fenced-in area as us.

"What the hell are we doing here?"

The scruffy guy moves through the piles like a pro. "You ever heard of a Golden Cap?"

"What?" I don't have the energy for this shit.

"Magical Maui Mushrooms?"

Magical Maui Mushrooms? C'mon kid. These are urban legends. The kinds of things teenagers tell each other when they're trying to impress their friends. Those don't exist. *Right?*

"These aren't Golden Caps, but they'll do."

Duper plucks a skinny stem from a hardened cow patty and tosses it in his bag, then grabs another, more perfect specimen from within, holding the chosen mushroom up for me to see.

It's long and slender, the stem slightly curved, pale white and brittle from being in the sun a day or so already. The cap is like a tiny little umbrella, like the tip of a penis, dried and cracked along the edges revealing an odd bluish-green discoloration within. He turns it over to show me the stem, and in the place where he had picked it moments before and holds it now, it is turning a deep bright blue.

"See the color? That's the psychoactivity."

I turn, and like a veil has been lifted from my childlike eyes, I see them. Hundreds of them. Maybe thousands. Tiny little caps, glimmering in the afternoon sun, clumped together on cow patties the size of a folded brown leather boot. Some of the patties have forty mushrooms growing from them, at least. Maybe more.

"Holy shit."

"Yup!" Duper giggles. He couldn't be more proud. He stands in the field like a champion farmer with the best local produce at the farmer's market, all of which he gets for free.

Suddenly, the synapses to my brain spark, fry, and collapse. My facial expression registers something equivalent to a stroke.

"Wait," I feel myself blurt out. "Psychedelic mushrooms grow in cow dung?" Reality slowly sinks in.

"Pretty cool, huh?"

I don't know what he's talking about, but I am suddenly cognizant of a strange new reality that cows might actually be psychoactive animals that aren't really stupid after all. They're just tripping all the time. Chris and his scuzzy friend practically dance between them and their land mines, dipping over to pluck their prized finds from their shitty existence before swinging on to the next patty as

their trash bags quickly fill up with skinny white mushroom dicks and cow manure.

"Ugh." I can feel myself wretch all over again.

"Ain't you ever shroomed before?"

"No."

"Never?"

I thought I made myself clear on the matter, but I guess not, so I confirm.

"No. Never."

"Ah, shit man." He pauses, looking at me queerly. "You want to?"

A wave of insecurity rolls over me. "There's like a statute of limitations on this, right? For old people? I mean, for like taking psychoactive chemicals and such. Right?"

He's gotten used to laughing at me. "No, man."

"So… What's it like?"

"Ahhh… It's the greatest thing ever. It's like, all of time embraces you in a warm hug, and takes your mind into another galaxy, where you can look back, and reflect on your existence here, man. And it's, like… *magical.*"

Ironically, this sounds exactly like the transformative experience I was seeking on this journey to begin with. I might not have found the Fountain of Youth, or even reached the Seven Pools of Ohio, but perhaps the Road to Hana has not been without fruit, even if that fruit was born out of the excrement of a heifer.

"Alright," I shrug, somewhat indifferently.

"Brother, you're in for the time of your life."

He pulls about a dozen or more mushrooms from his bag and brushes the dried clumps of cow turds from the bottom, laying each one in a row on the grass. Fourteen in total. Then, he rips a square out of his plastic bag and wraps the mushrooms inside, tying them up in a bow. He hands me the small care package of stank fecal mushrooms then pulls his bag open and continues harvesting the field. And the cows, copacetic in this arrangement, add a fresh batch of manure just as quickly as the old has been sifted through. And as the sun moves across the late afternoon sky the white fungal umbrellas begin to wither and

fade so the trio throw themselves into a manic harvesting fit to procure as many mushrooms as they possibly can before the very thing they've come to gather expires right in front of their eyes. Taken by the very thing that brings them life in the first place: the warmth of the sun. And standing here, in this field of cow shit and fungus, I become keenly aware of an amazing cycle of life: from birth to death to rebirth, from fertilizer to flower to food, and from cud to bullshit to enlightenment; this is one weird world we're living in.

*   *   *   *   *

We get back late. After the plucking of dung-cicles from cow patties in a remote pasture off the road to Hell, we drive back in the pitch black of night without a single streetlamp to guide us along our winding path, only the flashing brake lights of whatever car or truck happens to be in front of us for that brief amount of time before we pass them. We're in the outside lane, again, the one where mere inches to the right of the paved road there is a seventy meter drop to the rocky beachhead below, but we're not driving in it because Duper is overly intoxicated or out of control, but because this is the designated lane for people driving in this direction in this country, so help us, God. And we're passing people! On the inside lane though, my only relief. Fortunately, no one in their right mind is driving out this way this late so the oncoming lane is practically empty. Shockingly, there's a heavy amount of traffic leaving Hana at this time of night, no doubt all tourists wiped out from all of their recent hiking excursions and waterfall watching. I know I am. I'm stoned as all get out and paranoid as hell of the seven giant trash bags of mushrooms we have smashed into the trunk and the back seat of the car between me and Chris. And I swear this tiny little Korean P.O.S. is about a blink away from taking a turn too wide and tumbling right over the side of the canyon if Duper doesn't slow his ass down on this thirty-seven-mile, hair-pinned, one-lane road, and our only way back to *Paella*, or wherever the hell they're taking me right now, on the other side of the mountain.

I ride with my head out the window for the last half of the trip to get some air and am bombarded by the sweet fragrance of lush tropical

flowers, giving me something to concentrate on besides my sea-sick stomach the whole way home. At long last, we arrive safely in the small town of Paia according to the sign, where they direct me to a bar to catch a ride. A local fisherman from Kahului hears us talking in the parking lot and offers to give me a lift, and though I'm happy to stand in one unmoving place for a moment, I'm just as eager to get back to the resort, and I gladly accept. I'm a little nervous about this pocketful of mushrooms in my shorts as I hop in beside the old man, but the overwhelming smell of fish from his successful afternoon makes me forget as my stomach turns over itself. The fisherman has long white hair and beads braided into a long strand down the front, almost like an Indian, and he seems keen on hearing about my day, so I speak as much as I can without telling him about the mushrooms, or exhaling on him, which makes it a very short-lived conversation. Back in town, he drops me at a gas station and bids me adieu with an "Aloha," and I consider giving him some mushrooms but I think better of it and offer him a hundred bucks instead. He refuses.

"Just take it. I don't have any change."

"No worries, bro. You have a nice trip."

He drives off, leaving me in thought. Did he know about the mushrooms the whole time? Or was that just an expression?

Ten minutes later a taxi pulls in for gas and I convince him to drive me to Ka'anapali. He's irritable but accepts. It's gonna be another hour and seventy-two dollars, but I don't care. I'm eager to get home.

When I slam the door closed the cab driver looks at me with that same disgruntled look I usually give cab drivers in other major cities. He wrinkles his nose, cracks the windows, and takes off down 380 to 30, where I hope the sea air will help wash off some of this rancid vomit, dried sweat, and cow shit smell I've been emitting for the better part of the day. It's dark outside, so I hope he can't tell that I look equally as bad as I smell. Or worse.

He drops me off, I swipe my card, and he speeds off as quickly as any taxi in Paradise has ever sped anywhere. I chalk it up to a busy night, even though the hotel lobby looks especially dead, and I nod past the doorman who kindly nods back. Finally, I'm back on home turf. I

head directly to the tiki bar without a second thought. Directly toward the tiki bar, and Mena.

Mena. *Oh no.* I stop just before I hit the outdoor enclave, and turn around. I can't see her like this. I need a bath. I look and smell putrid. I duck inside before anyone sees me and I race to the room. Within minutes, I'm back en route to the tiki, my breath no longer the flavor of sausage bile. Or weed smoke, I don't think. It's hard to tell when you're this high. That was some good shit, I did that hours ago. But I'm slowly coming down. The shower helped. And brushing my teeth. And the added adrenaline from walking around with a hundred or so dollars' worth of illicit psychedelic mushrooms in your pocket, that'll get you going.

I perch at my usual spot at the bar, usual meaning three nights running, with the cheeriest grin on my face in fifteen years and just as quickly my stomach sinks. The bartender turns, and it's not Mena. She's much taller. It's not her at all. Instead, it's some broad-chinned, thin-lipped angry-looking bitch standing in her place, with the same sweat-soaked tee, and the same dirt brown saggy tits. She's like Mena, but in twenty years, and I am quick to realize it does not look good on her. She fake smiles at me with her gray teeth and I have to look away I'm so overcome.

"Can I get you something?"

"Umm... "

I'm the only person here. Me and another guy. Some rock-solid model type at the other end of the bar. He's hugging on some bimbo. And there's a table full of jackasses around the other side, by the pool. But on my end it's just me, that's it.

"I'm not sure."

"Here's a menu. Take your time." She bats her eyes at me and I look at the menu just to have something else to glare at.

God, I hope Mena walks out from the main restaurant with a bucket of ice or bag of limes or those sweet little Maraschino cherries she drops in all my Mai Tai's like tiny red balls, always two of them, and always with some phallic orange spear and a sword poking me in the eye as I'm trying to get my fucking drink on. "Where is she," I wonder aloud.

And like that, Mena rounds the other side of the bar. I didn't even know there was another side of the bar. All I ever care about is this spot and Mena. And here she is. The legendary seductress and mythical bartender.

"Hey, Frank."

I never told her that. Did I? Maybe she deciphered the chicken scratch whirl of my signature, but that's impossible. She must've looked up my room number for the bill. She knows where I sleep. She may have seen me nude. Wait, has she? Or did she just see me puke? So many thoughts race through my head.

"Hey."

"You get home okay last night?" She's mocking me. Her sense of humor's so biting and cute. I both dread and ceaselessly wonder how much she knows.

"Yeah."

I meet her eyes and she smiles across at me when the taller abrasive one interrupts.

"You decide on something?"

"Uhhh…" I refer to the menu again like's it's got all the answers I need, only I can't even read the thing at the moment so it does me no good.

"I got it," Mena announces, yanking the menu from my hand. "We got Myers back in."

Oh, Mena. Mena saves the day.

A jingle of ice. A splash of rum. Fruit juice cocktail. The secret sauce. A drip of dark rum. It sticks to a napkin. To the lips. Perfection.

"Thanks, babe."

That was too forward. She smiles anyway, picks up a rack of dirty glasses giving me a perfect view of her ass, and whatever that symbol's supposed to be on her lower back, and she's off… disappearing around the corner. The tall one stares at me with nothing but contempt. She's probably my age. She sees right through me.

I slide off the barstool and mosey around the corner to see how far this tiki hut goes.

It doesn't. It ends just like I thought, but there's a back door the wait staff can exit through to carry stuff like empty ice bins and racks

of dishes back to the main kitchen, across a different bridge on the other side, which Mena crosses now. I'm ten steps behind her when she disappears inside the restaurant, leaving me hanging on the back patio area, hovering with my cocktail like an unwanted party guest at some other family's Thanksgiving.

Damnit. So close. But what was I going to do when I caught her? What am I trying to accomplish with all of this? I leave in two days, back to the mainland, back to the empty apartment and the job searching and the shitty writing gigs and day jobs I have to take on to get by. And, hopefully, another one of these will come along, and I'll hop on a plane to some other corner of the planet, and maybe there I'll find whatever it is they want me to write about. Whatever it is I'm supposed to be looking for. Or maybe I've already found it. Maybe that's why I'm here right now.

About the time my stream of consciousness runs out of things to say, she walks back out, empty-handed, floating across the patio back to her station at the tiki hut. I catch her by the arm as we cross the lit bridge and when she twirls around I'm suddenly uncertain of what I want to say.

She doesn't seem all that alarmed.

"Hey!"

"Hey."

I've run out of things to talk about already. She looks at me, patiently waiting.

"Your drink okay?"

My hesitation must have warranted this.

"Yeah, yeah. I was just wondering, umm… Would you like to go out? To, like, get a drink later…? With me?"

That came out all wrong. Jesus, I haven't done this in forever. What did I do last night when all my inhibitions were down? Tonight, I'm a total wreck. My insecurities fluster me. Why am I so insecure? I'm a grown-ass man, damn it. I've been dating women my whole life. I love women. I've loved a few of them, at least. A couple of them, anyway. But love doesn't always turn out the way you think it will. And look at me now, I'm a twitching nervous wreck. I'm standing here in front of some thirty-something-year-old girl embarrassing myself like a

fucking fool. This was so much easier before I gave a shit, and now that I realize I do, I know I'm screwed.

"Are you high?"

"Who? Me? *No*. Why?"

"Oh." She looks disappointed. She knows. Everybody knows. "You look high as shit."

I can't hide it. There's no need to anyway.

"You're right. I am."

"Oh my God... Did you just lie to me?"

"No."

"You just did it again!"

"I'm sorry, I really didn't mean to, it's just... I'm old. I don't do things like this, but..." My voice trails off. I know what I want to say, but there's no mature way to say it. I'm a twelve-year-old boy, sitting on the bleachers beside Natalie Cartwright, staring at her blossoming rosebuds as she searches me with those eyes caked with clumpy mascara, while I will up the courage to say the way I really feel so I can reach my hand up her shirt, or run the risk of blowing my chance forever.

"But... *what...?*"

I take a long and thoughtful pause before I say it as plainly as I can deliver. "I want you to get a drink with me."

Once again, here I stand, prematurely exposed before a woman I've only just met, emotionally bare and broken. She can see I'm already ruined and we haven't even kissed.

Mena stands there, smirking that all-knowing, all-seeing, forget-about-it smirk of hers. She bites her bottom lip, reminding me she's only a few spins around the globe past her teenage years, and can probably chalk my emotional embarrassment up as 'cute.' I'm pathetic. But God she's beautiful. I lose myself in her eyes only to blink with an early epiphany: I don't even know this girl, but I'm pretty sure I'm falling for her.

She looks around the empty patio, stalling, searching for ways to get out of this, reasons that haven't yet come to her to explain why she can't come and where else she's supposed to be. *"But next time, I swear..."* and if she can just figure out a way to hold out for two more

days then I'll never see her again and that'll be it, folks. That's all she wrote. A relationship damned before it ever got started. All because I couldn't shut my fuckin-

"Alright… give me, like, fifteen minutes, and I'm off."

"Oh! Ok… *Great*!"

Tamper expectations. Don't sound so desperate, or excited. My inner jockey attempts to grab me by the reins before I blow all my momentum.

"On one condition."

I knew it. It's always something. The perfect deal is always too good to be true.

"You got any more weed?"

The deer-in-headlights look on my face gives me away. I got so high I never actually got any weed.

"Shit."

"No? I thought you got high."

"I did. With some friends."

"Friends, huh?"

"Yeah, but I just smoked with them. I didn't buy anything. I forgot."

"They got any more?"

I shrug. "Probably."

"Why don't you call them?"

"I don't have their number."

"What kind of friends are these exactly?"

"Just some people I met."

"Oh… right. On your *vacation*."

I can hear the disappointment in her voice and I wonder if she'll still come out on that date. I know she won't. What reason would she have to go out with an old bastard like me?

And then it hits me. I light up like a Christmas tree.

"I don't know if you'd be interested, but I might have something a little… stronger."

"Stronger? Than weed? What does that even mean?"

"Hallucinogenic mushrooms."

"What? Shut up…"

I stare at her blankly, purposefully masking any sign of expression to maximize the seriousness of my proposal. We are going to travel to distant galaxies together if only she'll come along for the ride.

Her eyes widen with anticipation.

"Nuh-uh. Are you serious?"

I pull the tied makeshift plastic bag from my pocket, though in and of itself it reveals nothing. I might as well have a turd in there, as that's what it smells like.

She never doubts me for a minute.

"But how did you…?"

"It's a long story. Meet me here in fifteen and I'll tell you all about it."

I slug my drink back, only finishing about half, and hand it to Mena before abruptly marching off toward the lobby like this was all some sort of secret agent rendezvous that should never be spoken of again, or at least the real-life version of that clichéd movie scene.

Mena looks at the glass and glares at me, confused.

"You can come back to the bar and finish your drink if you like."

I pause, busted.

"I know. I'm going to pee."

Nice recovery, I think. Or maybe not, I dunno. Maybe that was a little too forward.

She doesn't care. These girls today. They're raw. They don't give a fuck. I think I like that in a woman. But she looks pissed. Maybe I'm reading her all wrong.

Fifteen minutes later we're skipping in the sand, searching for a quiet place on the beach for our night to begin. She's got pot in her purse from a busboy she claims gets nothing but indica fire, and I've got mushrooms in my pocket I got from some eighteen-year-old hippie with fecal matter under his fingernails. Every time I put my hand in my shorts pocket it comes out smelling like shit. I can't imagine what that car smells like by now. Or their apartment. Or wherever those vagabonds plan on storing seven trash bags full of cow crap.

We dip behind a catamaran rental hut and follow a well-maintained boxwood shrub to a private concrete bench hidden behind a massive, sprawling interwoven tree, of which species I have no idea. I feel like a child again, nervously hiding from my mother as I knowingly do something she wouldn't approve of, hoping not to get caught, but knowing that even if I do it could still be worth it in the end. Or at least I hope.

We sit on the bench together and I pull the black plastic baggie from my pocket before tearing it open to reveal the bluish-white stems and caps inside. Most of the caps have broken apart from the stems, leaving nothing but dried sticks and buttons to be consumed. Unsure of what to do, exactly, I offer the bag to her in hopes of guidance.

"You want one?"

"No. I'm good." She sparks her bowl, taking a content hit before blowing it playfully in my face.

I look into the ripped black bag with uncertainty, and then as if suddenly possessed with someone else's appetite for destruction, I reach in and pull a cap and two long stems from the bag and eat them. They taste awful. They're chewy and slimy and gummy and shitty and I have no idea what to expect but somehow this doesn't seem like enough and I never want to do this again so I take two more out of the bag and gag them down, too.

She wrinkles her nose in delight. "Alright! Someone's getting down tonight!"

I almost choke in response, and I look at the baggie of shriveled skinny mushrooms in my lap with disgust and for a second I hate her. There's easily ten more of the suckers in there. Plus God knows what else. Crumbs of cow shit, perhaps? It's hard to tell what's what. All I can think as I'm chewing is those kids are literally getting rich selling bullshit.

And my mind is racing right now. Racing for all the right things to say. Racing to impress Mena with my vast collection of knowledge and talents. And a quick retort is about as far away as she is from me, and so I grasp at the first thing that pops in my head and throw it out for good measure.

"I thought you were going to do it with me…" I try to play it as cool as I can, despite the ridiculous amount of unintentional innuendo in that statement. There's shit in my teeth, I can feel it. My breath can't get any worse. I need to fix this. Say something smart. "The guy that gave them to me said it would take us into galaxies unknown, where we can look back on our existence here on Earth, and reflect." I pause dramatically, for emphasis. "So don't make me eat them all by myself."

"So what's your deal exactly that you come out here alone, this week in particular, only to spend your time buying mushrooms and solo tripping with some girl you just met?"

"Does that seem weird to you?"

"No." The playful sarcasm draws from her lips with a hint of southern charm and I wonder where she's from.

"Good. Me neither."

I figure this is her whole spiel before she dives in and shares all of her intimate secrets with me, but no, she keeps grilling me instead.

"So, what are you running from?"

"What? Nothing. Who said I was running from anything?"

"Everybody that comes to Paradise is running from something. I was just wondering what you're running from?"

"Does that mean you're running from something?"

"Nope. I stopped running. That's why I'm still here."

I look at her. I can't compete with whatever level she just woke me up to. I stand before her, dumbstruck, searching for words that I hope will trigger from the most eloquent part of my speech patterns to say-

"*Cool.*"

I nod, unsure of what to say next, or whether or not it was my turn to speak or hers, or whether I ever answered her question, whatever it was, and wondering if I should eat another mushroom or two just to make sure they work or have I already had my fair share? How fucked up am I going to get tonight? How fucked up have I already gotten? How far down this rabbit hole am I willing to go before there's no turning back?

Mena's busy packing another bowl so I go for it, reach in the bag and gag down another two caps. This certainly gets her attention, though she's been looking at me funny ever since we sat down.

"So where did you get those things again?"

"Oh! I forgot to tell you! I went to Hana today. You ever been?"

She glares at me like I just asked if she's ever heard of America, then goes back to packing her bowl, suddenly skeptical of the yarn I'm prepared to tell.

"So, you went to Hana and you just happened to come back with a giant bag of 'shrooms? How does that happen exactly?"

"Well, apparently, they grow in cow shit."

"Yeah, I know. So... You drove all the way to Hana to dig through cow shit?"

I hunch down, nervous to be seen by other people. "No... we didn't go into Hana. We just sorta passed it before we turned off and stopped."

"Who's we?"

"Oh, these guys I met on the way. For a while I thought they were going to murder me, you know, but they turned out to be really nice guys."

"Oh yeah? Who were they? Like, locals? Or from someplace else?" Mena sounds nervous. She's noticeably more eager for answers than before.

"Oh definitely local. Hey! I wonder if you know him! You ever heard of a kid named Duper?"

"Ahh...." Like a balloon depleted of its air, the tension within her diffuses. "Duper's the best. Everybody knows Duper. And Chris was there, I'm sure. And JC? Long hair, kind of creepy."

"Yup. JC was there."

"That's so awesome you met them! Duper's great. I love him."

"Yeah, so.... Question: How did Duper get to be called 'Duper,' exactly?"

Mena bursts out laughing. It's the type of laughter that causes milk or snot to fly out of your nose if there is any. In her case, there's only smoke.

72

"Ohhhh, Duper." She exhales it like there's an anthology on the subject, but says no more.

"So, do you know?"

"It's a long story. You wouldn't believe me if I told you."

"Try me."

She holds her bowl contemplatively, then puts it to her lips. "Maybe another time. Tell me about your day."

She takes her hit and I regale her with the turbulent story of my adventures to Hana and before I know it she chomps through four caps and a couple chewy shit sticks like they're grandma's oatmeal cookies. I politely offer her the last few, which she scarfs down, and I immediately regret it, having secretly hoped that I'd get the last one.

And we sit and discuss and smoke and laugh and flirt within our cozy little hideout behind the tree until suddenly I am overcome with a wave of nausea I haven't felt since a couple hours ago, at least.

"Oh my God, I might be sick…"

"Are you okay?"

And without warning I bowl over, grappling with my stomach which is clenched in a knot so tight surely the only thing to do is gut me like a fish and let this pain within be free. I feel as though my bowels are about to burst, leaving whatever's left to seep out through every orifice of my body. I stand to get my bearings and immediately double over again, unable to handle this agony any longer. This nauseating tidal wave that pulses through me unleashes such a powerful urge within my gut that I believe I am about to unloose a diarrheal experience upon my shorts when instead I unleash a belch that so deeply resonates from my being that it sounds akin to a mating bullfrog, and immediately I feel better.

"Holy shit."

I try and catch my breath, a need for oxygen arising from deep within. That feeling was excruciating in every way up until now, now it has subsided and I am slowly approaching bliss. Warm waves roll through my brain, lapping inside me with a magnetic current that charges every electron within my soul. I've never felt so calm. So warm as now. Everything around me is crystal clarity clear.

And when she smiles her eyes twinkle like the stars, and I can't help but fall in love.

*   *   *   *   *

Bonfires of life percolate from metal barrel tops and pyres of wood carried to the beach by human shadows now dancing around them in a steady tribal beat, which emanates from somewhere beneath the surface like a volcanic rhythm that only those most attuned to the land can hear. Like the circadian rhythms of Mother Earth, I can feel them pulsating through me from the ground up, and if I let them, they will surge throughout my being like an electronic socket of power that explodes my heart into my veins and my mind into my nerve endings until every touch is cerebral, every sight is more colorful and vivid, every sound more nuanced, and every thought a deeper exploration into the infinite emotional chambers of the mind.

I feel fucking great right now. More alive than I've felt in years. Spiritually cleansed. Vehemently purified, from the inside out. I can breathe deeper than I've ever breathed. The neurons in my brain are charged and firing like battleships at war with one another, tickling the mind in ecstasy as it explores new territory across the synaptic sea. I've been purged at long last, that belch a sacrifice from the bowels of my being to the heavenly Gods, so I can exhale the waste that fills my lungs and inhale new atomic particles that will imbue me with this spiritual celebration called Life.

"Whooooooa..." My mind is reeling.

The crowd gyrates to the thundering bass line in a spectacle of strobing lights, streaming tracers, and sweaty bodies. Flickering lights. Echoing screams. Wild abandon. Deranged ghouls. Snarling beasts. Ferocious bloodsuckers. At any moment, the fiends will surely turn on each other and begin to feast, and my appetite is growing by the second.

She looks at me, a maddening grin chasing across her face, and her eyes swell with light before her pupils are absorbed back into their darkened abyss, back into the meaningful wells she peered from before,

74

yet even more knowledgeable, inviting, and enchanting than ever before.

"Where are we?"

"Just keep walking."

"Is this some sort of…. Circus?"

"No."

"Is it a *rave*?"

She looks at me and laughs, some maniacal witch-like thing of the sort I would imagine haunts Dorothy's poppy field dreams.

"What is it? Where are we?" I'm desperate to know. The lack of not knowing encroaches on my satisfaction like an oil spill on a swan's back. My whole world is going dark.

"Please…" I beg.

She takes my hand and pulls me close as she continues to tromp down the beach.

"It's just some people listening to music."

It's what? I turn to look, and sure enough, fading in the dark but illuminated by the flaming barrel are six or seven people standing in a circle, calmly hanging out.

Impossible. Moments before I was entranced on the front lines of Club Paradiso, surging with the crowd to the exploding bass lines of subwoofers on the verge of imploding inside their own casing. I was engulfed. Not by the flames, or the sand, or the sea, but in People. In dancers. In movement. In glow sticks. In the music. In lightness and darkness and beauty and fear and makeup and nudity and obscenity. It was fucking Burning Man back there and we were right in the middle of it. Engulfed in the entire scene. And then, it was all gone, as she grabbed me by the hand and the colorful display of music that filled my head and the hallucinations that filled my vision seconds before disappeared like a momentary mirage that faded into the blurry night. I clench my hand and am happy to feel that hers is bound tightly within. How long I've been doing this I can't be sure.

"Don't worry, I'm right here with you."

And then I see it, there before me like a puzzle that's been in pieces so long that it's impossible to see the whole picture until it's complete. When I finally stand back and admire it in all its magnificent glory, it's breathtaking. I stand there, clenching her hand, watching the ocean as it rolls out to sea. Watching as a few storm clouds swirl around the moon until I can make out faint strings in the sky, magically lulling the ocean forward and back, repeatedly unfolding upon itself like an escalator's loop until the end of eternity. Each wave begins somewhere on the horizon, slowly working its way to the sand until it has gathered enough momentum to form a foamy fist upon which it strikes down on the beach. And as it rolls back out, it is clear to me, a new formation out in the waves… a vision of such magnitude I can hardly believe it, or the implications of what it can mean. As each white-capped wave rolls over the next, a sea of stairs arises toward the horizon, calling me toward it, a bridge into the skies, an escalator toward the cloudy heavens where I can finally achieve everything I ever dreamed I could achieve. This could lead me toward everything I ever wanted to be. All I have to do is go.

I turn to share my new purpose and wondrous vision with my new love, but I'm alone. Where did she go? I see flashes of seafoam and seaweed and strange faces and fire pits and my feet are moving beneath my body but my eyes can't see to tell them where to go, and voices circle around me, outside the ones in my head, and as nervous anticipation about my whereabouts rises within me I can't catch my breath. And as panic sets in, I run.

I run down the beach, lost, hopeless, alone, searching the blurred impressionistic faces of everyone I pass, strutting up to each one of them and grabbing them, bending them over forthright to inspect them and whatever they might be doing before fleeing the scene to find my next victim. I know who I am looking for, but I am lost, in mind and spirit, and by what circumstance I can't remember, but I know that I will not be complete until she is here with me again. But she is not to be found, and the stormy clouds in the sky block the moon and the shadows of the world form around me until they are too frightening to investigate, and I stop. But the world around me has been spun like a top, and I'm hanging on for dear life.

I drop despondently into the sand and allow my mind to slowly unwind from its tightly spun and heavily tangled coil before the spring is finally sprung. Nature's music whistles above as the wind makes reedy synthesizers out of the palm trees. My hands reach down into the sand, once a cloying nuisance, now a soft sedimentary quilt, and what begins as a light exfoliation of the palms along the sandy surface of Mother Earth quickly transforms into scooping piles of watery sand from deep wells on the beach dump-truck style and sifting through it, completely transfixed on repeatable actions and form, painfully ignorant of the transformative healing powers of nature, the beach, the ocean, and my emergent oneness of being with it all. And I keep digging. Digging, clawing, scratching, mining, and no longer am I thinking about the rolling staircase out to sea, or my aloneness, or of nature, but of this sand. This sand that tickles against my fingers. This sand that scratches my skin warm like I'm in a cozy bubble bath. At this point, I'm less likely to end up wading out into the ocean to deliver myself to fate on the Stairway to Heaven as I am to end up in China, through a tunnel I've dug with my own bare hands.

"What'cha doing?"

I look up and Mena's smiling down at me, watching over me, like a mother watches her playful son. There's no one else around, as I imagined there might be, and her face is in silhouette from the white light of the full moon. I don't know where she's been, maybe nowhere, maybe everywhere. It doesn't matter now that she's with me again. She reaches down for me and I rise.

"Come on." She takes my sand-covered hand and away we go, jogging, *sprinting* down the beach. My toes clench into the soft, sticky muck left from the recently lowered tide. Our feet stomp through the damp mushy earth, leaving not delicate footprints, but dual clods of trampled ground like massive hoof prints from a frightful, sordid beast. I don't know how long we've been here. Or how long I've been anywhere, on Earth or in this Heaven. All I know is here, in this moment: her movements, her odor, her hair as it blows behind her, her strong galloping legs as they carry her swiftly and endlessly down the dark and deserted coast. I chase her down the beach as if it's my sole duty on Earth. It's the only time I've felt truly alive in my long and lonely life.

And then, like somebody switched off the light, I realize I can't see. The fire from the trash can rages a half-mile down the beach, and here we are, completely alone, panting in the cool salty midnight air, lit only by the reflecting light of a nearly full moon. Van Gogh's clouds are all gone. I wonder if they were ever there to begin with. She stops to wait for me to catch up, and as I catch my breath I realize that for once in my life there's no place I'd rather be, wherever we are. Wherever this is. But in this happiness a simple question of doubt can't help but creep in and taint this otherwise euphoric journey of body and mind: *Why me?*

Why me circles inside my head like a repeated loop of my least favorite jingle. Why me, and not some other Tourist/Reporter/Fan/Asshole/Drunk at the tiki bar that might have given her the same barstool treatment I gave her? Maybe she did? Maybe she does, every other week? Maybe I'm not that special after all, and neither is she? Maybe I'm just one more in a long line of the same and if so why do I care so badly whether or not I get to lie down here in the sand and kiss this girl when I know that's exactly what I want to do. I'm already jealous of every man that ever kissed her before me and every man that might do it after. I hate them with everything I have left to hate them with. And I desire her with everything else.

I look out and it's completely calm. The ocean's calm. The wind is calm. The night sky above me twinkles like a giant curtain has been hung over the world and poked repeatedly with a needle, allowing the faintest twinkles of light to escape from the larger, brighter star behind it, patiently awaiting the dawn of a new day when the curtain can be drawn and the sun can keep shining like the bright and shining star it is and always will be, until it dies. And as I stare into the night sky, my mind grows calm. My thoughts slow down just long enough for me to be able to decipher the space that exists between one thing and another. Me and her. The sky and the ocean. My feet and the sand. This permeating feeling of ecstasy and the knowledge that I will come down, eventually. I let my mind run free, and it unwinds like a spool of thread into the wind, ripping away my cares, my fears, all the pent-up energy and rage I ever felt toward screaming fans and basketball tournaments and rotten assignments and overcooked eggs and nagging wives and gold-toothed maids and judgmental taxi drivers and video buffering and lost cell phones... All of it zips down the hallway of my conscience and I free myself to completely release my mind. My head surges with a powerful intensity of knowledge, power, and strength. My black eyes twinkle beneath the starlit constellations either real or imagined, glowing in the dark blue sky like intangible lines across the universe. And in my perfect decision-making prowess, the almighty everything becomes as crystalline as the tiny grains of glass I tread upon. I know what I want. I know what I need.

She lies down under a palm tree, in a unique little hammock that seems to be there just for her. Maybe it is. Maybe it's hers. Perhaps she lives here, in this quaint, cozy little beach house behind us. I sit beside her, on a small patch of grass at the base of the tree, and watch her swing in the moonlight. It's quiet except for a few drunken wolves howling a half-mile down the beach. But I don't mind. I don't pay any attention to them. Only to her. Only to my beautiful Mena. I stroke her hair as she lies in the hammock and I profess my love to her.

"I love you." A distant wave crashes. And another. They are the only response. Maybe it's better this way.

"Do you ever, like, imagine a time when you didn't exist?"

"What?"

"Or maybe a time when you do exist, but it's like, you're looking in on yourself, like watching what you do, only it isn't you… it's someone else… You're not in control of it. You're just there. Like someone else's puppet, you're just hanging on for dear life. You know?"

Like the Road to Hana… This is some mind-bending shit.

"I guess…" I'm not sure what else there is to say. Maybe nothing. Maybe everything. Lucky for me, she picks up the slack.

"I don't know…. It's… It's a big world. Bigger than you and I will ever know. All the little… the little dark places… like the crevices in our brain… some of which we're not even using until… until they're stimulated… And once activated those parts of our brain… those parts of the world… it's like we can't go back. You can't go back to the way it was. Just like history, I guess. It happens. It's activated. It's now. It's happening.. and then… It's gone. Right? You can't redo it. You could never repeat it, exactly. You can't recapture history once it's gone. Even now, at this moment, we could never redo it. All we can do is just, like… keep going. Through it all. You know? You. Me. We all… We exist… Until we don't… But that doesn't mean it didn't happen. It still happened. Even if it doesn't last. Even if it's gone. Even if there's nobody there to remember it, or write it down, or witness it at all, it still happened. Right?"

I'm speechless. "Of course," is the best I come up with.

"But… How do you know? How can you be sure? What if we don't remember, right? *That's* what I'm most afraid of. What if… you know... What if we're doomed to forget?"

Now I really don't know what to say. She's more fucked up than I am, that much is clear. I keep stroking her hair and whisper softly.

"You okay?"

She lets out a long resigned sigh and a little white lie. "Don't listen to me. It's just the shrooms."

We sit. It's quiet. Our minds race on though our mouths do not, self-doubting ourselves into submission so that we do not embarrass ourselves any more than we already have.

"What about *you*?" She asks. That puts me on defense. Smart thinking. Always on her toes. Now, what do I say? What do I say now?

"What about me?"

Put it back on her, there you go.

"What do you think… about life?"

I can't play this game forever.

"Honestly, it's a crockpot full of shit."

"No! That's the thing. It's not! It's *beautiful*. It's amazing… Can't you see it? This entire world is a *Miracle* and everyone in it… It's miraculous we're even here. How we've adapted, and how we've changed. And just think about how much potential we have, all of us… The human race… It's *extraordinary*."

As she searches for meaning in her own words, I silently listen with the knowledge that those words don't mean anything to me. Not anymore. Maybe they could have, I don't know. But that word, *miracle*, it hangs there, clenched in my forethought, and my entire life flashes before my eyes. Tiny glimpses, realizations, patterns, and shadows strobing between my neurons, firing throughout my body… my entire world goes radiantly numb… my brain sizzles… and I clench my eyelids tightly closed… my shoulders fall silent and I lie down in a hardened knot.

Miracle. There's no such thing. Only illusion. Or delusion, if you're brave enough to call it that. The Miracle of Life. A Miracle of Love. A Miracle Worker. These are all farce. Made-up, fictitious lies told to children to keep them from withering on the vine like an early grape, absorbing all the nutrients too fast so that by harvest time they're infected and covered in mold. We're no miracle. We're the mold rotting over this beautiful land, slowly infecting it with our greed and our disease. We're the parasite that's eating the overripe berry flesh and hatching our eggs all over it until our maggots destroy the whole fucking planet.

Slowly, I awaken, but I am not fully awake. I am asleep, but I am not dreaming. Gradually, I lift myself from my bed, stepping out of my body and into a new realm, and I turn within myself so that I can see my likeness, face to face, lying on the ground, my other self lying peacefully asleep beside the hammock. Mena lies above me, curled inside herself like a blanket, in a little ball. She's the real miracle here, no question. A shooting star suddenly spirals through the sky. I marvel at the sight, then look back at my peaceful slumbering self. There I lie, completely asleep on the ground, eyes closed, hair windblown and sandy, but otherwise not as bad a shape as I expected. I look ten years younger than normal. Impossible, I tell myself. It's my imagination. I'm just high. I close my eyes to see what happens and in what seems like an instant, just as I begin to dissipate into the night fog, her hand touches mine and I awaken on the ground. Her skin is soft, not what I expected at all. She tugs me off the tuft of grass.

"C'mon. You fell asleep."

I rise and am awake, barely. But she's here, and she takes my hand and in the darkness of the early morning she escorts me back to reality.

And under the light of the moon, our arms intertwine to keep each other warm and I smile, and for the first time all night I realize that I am in pain. I've been smiling at her all night. Smiling so much my face hurts. It's literally killing me, the tiny muscles in my jaw and my cheeks, my embouchure and my chin. But there's no way I can stop. I love it here. It really is Paradise.

*   *   *   *   *

I don't sleep a wink. I lie in bed, tossing and turning, thinking and dreaming of words, colors, lights, shadows, movement, and stillness. I'm quiet yet frantic, trapped in my head yet unleashed from my body. Self-assured but self-doubting. The world is my oyster, but mine is filled with grit. But something blossoms inside, something warm and calming, an aura of light growing out of the empty part of my stomach, filling my abdomen with a lightness it has not known in some time. I rise from my bed and stretch; a cat has never stretched so well, much less me, a stiff-necked screen nerd who spends more time hunched over his thirteen-inch monitor tied to a Chinese built processor than with people, nature, and the world. But not anymore. Not after tonight. I can feel the energy flowing through my body in long pulsating bursts from my heart, sending electrical charges into the cortex of my brain. Everything is changing. Inside my bosom. Inside my loins. Inside my entire being. The palm trees sway in the night air, and I can hear the waves crashing on the beach, I can taste the smell of the sea salt air in a crisp refreshing way I have never experienced before. Usually, it's all rotten fish and seaweed, but now, something's different. It's sea breeze and coconut palms. The world is different. My life is going to be different. I don't just feel it, I *know* it. I'm certain of it. Is this because of *her*? Or is it that quarter bag of mushrooms I imbibed roughly ten hours ago? The sky lightens on the horizon, and a sagging palm tree frames the dawn's heavenly glow, and it draws me out through the sliding glass door, waving me onward, outside the confines of my stiff dark room, and into the breezy early morning air. The world, I think, is all mine.

But then *it* comes creeping back in. That which has paralyzed me for all of these years. That which remains buried slightly under the surface, dormant, hiding, waiting for moments like this, moments of opportunistic yearning for it to wiggle back in and unhinge all of my efforts until I become smothered in it. This self-doubt that coagulates within my confidence like leftover gravy on a sausage biscuit. And it's stifling.

I look out onto the ocean. I'm alone here, now, just me, the breeze, the soft granules of sand between my lumpy calloused toes, the crashing salty ocean on the unforgiving beach shore, and my self-doubt. The waves roll back and forth in front of me, no longer an escalator to the moon, but a soothing call and response between the earth and sea. I listen to the crash of the pounding waves against the rigid sand with every ounce of liquid muscle the ocean can muster, but the earth, unyielding and unwavering in its stead, stands firm. And so, the ocean recedes, sucks in, and pulls back, taking another deep breath as it gathers another surge of vitality to pounce once more upon its eternal foe, and as the shore lies dormant below, with playful bubbles popping out of cockle holes that percolate all the way down the coast, the heavy water crashes landward again.

With every recession of every wave, I look back in a flashback of my life dating back to the flat line of the horizon, the day of my birth, all the way to the slowly accumulating ripple that ends here, on the beach, washing across the fatty ankles of my swollen sunburned feet. Saltwater cures all, on the outside. But inside it dries you out, chokes you up, and makes you bleed. It can kill you. Ever pour salt in a wound? It hurts. That's what she did. When she left. Everything was going great, and then, like the waves at my feet, that which seemed in reach one moment, slipped out from under me, receding right back into the great blue sea, where other fish and opportunities swim aplenty for those with the right bait. But for a man that never learned to fish, an expert catch will never be made.

It was a decade ago, at least. The mind grows hazy after that amount of time, memories unclear, but we were together, that much is known. And we were happy. For endless days and sleepless nights. And the novel, that gnawing beast that welled within me year after year, my best work always forthcoming, my full potential forever percolating, like the cockles along the beach floor, and to this day unrevealed... It sputtered and spit and foamed at the mouth to be taken seriously, but the real meat, the real substance behind the venom was never sincere, and therefore the work, such as it was, never delivered. And so I caved.

Retreating into my head and my excuses and my warm covers, and the days grew shorter and the nights grew longer, and the drinks grew stiffer and the yelling grew louder and I grew colder and then, like two statuesque figures carved from ice, we were frozen in time with nowhere else to go. Our stone bodies maneuvered around the chessboard of our home in a game, orchestrating each play around our opponents' next move until one day I woke up and The Queen was gone. Our entire existence, a fading dream. The happy life we planned, now a failed business proposal between partners soured on each other and the business itself. And it sucked. To think you put your entire life into something, your life's work, the ten thousand hours to be a professional, your entire future, everything you've worked so hard to create between you and another person... You put that on the line only to have it walk right out the fucking door. On you. Or because of you. Or me. Or my novel, whatever.

Only it wasn't my novel. I know that now. I mean, maybe it was. It was shitty, there's no doubt. I worked on it day in and day out for six hundred and forty-three days, and if I can just go over it one more time, just a quick read through to make sure everything flows the way it should, I promise it will be the last time...

Only I haven't written a meaningful word of substance or even attempted a novel in over seven years. Everything is gibberish. Incomplete and inconclusive. Uninteresting and unimportant. So, I gave up. On both of them, the book and her. Not before publishing, of course. But the critics, the fans, the audience for my story, they weren't there. Nobody was there. Only me. Me and my voice, ringing out word after word, page after page, chapter after chapter. And for what? My own self-worth? Because if that book is the value of my worth than I am worthless. Or at least that's what I thought. I thought it was up to people to give you worth. Other, hardworking people. People who live their whole lives providing a worth of their own, either a service, or a product, or a skill of some sort that affords them the luxury of going to the bookstore, and checking out the bestseller's list, and buying my book. Or not buying my book, as the case turned out to be. Either way, the book was not bought, and my publisher left. And then she did, too. Without warning, or explanation. Without prolonging the inevitable.

She just left. And I was left, too. Left with these feelings of being worthless.

She didn't have to explain why. I always knew. I was expecting it from the first moment we ever met. I was batting out of my league since day one. I don't know how it started really, those kinds of details get murky when you're drowning in the muddy waters of denial and delusion, but there was a spark, and in no time flat it was decided: we were a thing, and we were gonna be a thing because our thing worked. And she was beautiful. I mean drop-dead beautiful. And then thoughts and ideas and emotions and responsibility and opportunity and money and time and experience and everything else you stick into the blender and frappe as soon as you say the words "I do" spilled out onto the desktops of our lives and we were forced to take a really good look and digest it all as we cleaned up the sticky mess. And when my book didn't sell, and I couldn't peel myself off the couch, and she couldn't peel herself away from work, the collective fruit of our labors eventually dried out and left us with nothing but the shaved peels of withered rind and the stench of rotten jam. And I, too, was forced to move on.

Maybe I was destined to be alone. Maybe all of this... these feelings, these fears, these biting realizations that I have known all along, run from and hid behind, reveal themselves to me now so that I can let them go, the way she let me go, disappearing forever from my life and being. Yet there were traces of her everywhere. The Fleetwood Mac album she left in my record collection. A sock with the pink toe-stitch in the bottom of the washing machine. The fine glassware she bought and told me to keep because she didn't feel like taking the time to box every little thing up in great detail. She wanted out. The pity I had wallowed in over my book was smothering her, and like the survivor she is, she climbed out gasping for air, never looking back at the ball and chain that had held her back for so long. And where she went, I can't be sure. She never said where, and I never went looking.

But now there's Mena. Beautiful, mysterious Mena. And for some reason, she's chosen me. I let the self-doubt wash away and take a moment's pride that I've even gotten this far, this fast. And with someone so deeply special as her. I have only just met her but feel with all of my being that we were destined to meet like this. To fall in love this way, and to continue our adventure together from this day forward. Finding our path together; however winding, so that we can reach the highest peaks that life has to offer in tandem.

There's cloud cover over the moon and I get a chill. It's not the cookie-cutter white circle of before, but a fuzzy oval in the sky, diffused behind a haze of sea smoke rising over the island. The sun quietly peeks its way through the overcast ceiling to shine greyly on the early morning joggers, the dawn to dusk beach hikers, and the 5 a.m. dog walkers, and as I yawn I come to realize I haven't slept a wink. I probably won't. I've got sand all over me.

I turn around and shuffle back to my room, slip back through the sliding glass door on the patio, and fall into bed, sand and all. I'm completely spent. I've never slept so soundly in my life.

4

Wednesday

I'm thirsty. My breath reeks. These are the first thoughts in my head as I awaken, quickly followed by *God there's a lot of sand in the bed* and *I wonder what time it is?* The sand doesn't bother me as much today. Nothing bothers me. I feel like I ate a bottle full of Valium and someone adjusted the brightness and saturation levels on the TV monitor to my soul so that everything seems just a tad more vibrant than before, and a new affection toward life wiggles over me and I am exhilarated.

Jesus. Either I'm still tripping or I've permanently altered the chemistry of my brain. It's like the collective information stimulating my brain is being inverted and submitted through a tiny funnel that plays like a backward playing record, and yet my hyper-computing mind analyzes and counter-adjusts this nonsensical input malfunction in mere milliseconds while it encodes each and every bit of sensory information it receives in order to spit it back out in a re-imagined re-interpreted version of a brighter, fuller existence. And if I really put my mind to it, which I'm prone to do in such a state, I rationalize that this feeling that I have is not the same as last night. It's different. As a whole, I just kinda feel... *different.*

I asked her out last night. We had such a great time together I just couldn't help myself. It was while we walked back down the beach from the hammock, we had been laughing non-stop all night, my cheeks are still sore we laughed so hard, and we had just come out of another one of our shared laughing fits when I looked at her, and she at me, and it was one of those perfect harmonious moments you can't even plan, and if I'd had a ring I might have proposed, but I didn't, so the proposal of dinner was all she got. And she grew nervous. The effects of the mushrooms were largely wearing off, and the tracers and radical visuals I had encountered earlier in the evening were all gone, and her face was clear as day. She asked why, and what's the point, knowing that my stay is only temporary, and this thing, whatever it is between us has thus far been perfect. Why add expectations and commitments and responsibilities to it? Why add titles and time cards and money and complications? Why can't it just be? And I knew why, but I couldn't say it, not again. It was a sobering moment, for both of us, but she eventually put her small hand in mine and agreed.

I feel like there's something else I should be doing. Something else of great importance that I should be taking into account during my stay, but as long as it doesn't impede on my day, I don't care. If it's something that important it will come to me. I want nothing ruining my day. Not today. The sun's shining. The waves are crashing along that beautiful white sandy beach. And I've got a date tonight with Mena. Who knows, maybe I was wrong. Maybe there are miracles after all.

"I think I'm going for a swim," I say aloud alone in my room to no one in particular.

And I do just that.

The ocean's a lot colder than I would have figured. Must be why all those kids are at the pool. But the beach is still nice. Hot. Sandy. Just like I remember it as a little boy. I burn my feet a little as I half jog from the spot where I lay my towel in the soft sand to the edge of the foamy water. That first touch, skin to tide, that nervous rush of dreaded cold, that surge of adrenaline as the chill rises up your ankles and through your legs and up your groin and into the pit of your stomach until you gasp for oxygen and relief before submerging yourself completely and letting your oneness with the earth and with nature and with the hot beating sun and the world around you reach divinity. All you have to do is lie back and float in sync with the universe. I close my eyes, raise my face to the sky, and soak the sun into the sea, myself a pillar, a conduit, a synapse between sky and water, sun and globe, ocean and galaxies, heavens and earth, life and death. My soul screams with the burning desire for a passionate life and well being. I want to live! For too long I have buried myself in the sorrowful sands of pity, drawn into my own well like a sinkhole, destined to fail beneath the emotional weight I carry. But now I am in love. Now I prepare myself for a selfless future where the real Miracles of the world will finally reveal themselves to me their simple pleasures so that I can discover the intricate nature and interconnectedness of all things: atoms, matter, and marvels.

Kerplunk! A wave swallows my legs out from under me and sends me crashing into shore. I hit the ocean floor elbow first, then face, before I'm flipped over and sucked back out to sea. I retaliate against the current as it drags me into the next set of waves and as I try to stand and get my footing amidst the slick retreating granules another wave topples over me. Then another. I can no longer feel the chill of the water, only the burning of the fibers in my muscles and my gasping for air as the power of the Gods I harnessed only moments before turns its angry hand against me, and I scream out "Shit!" and "Help!"

I go down again. By this point, I'm resolute that anyone and everyone on the beach is getting one hell of a good show out of this, yet nobody's doing a God damned thing to help. I'll probably survive this angry trip, but my ego won't. I feel the sand move from under my feet and my toes clench in, but like quicksand, my entire foot is enveloped and I'm instantly buried up to my ankles. Trapped. Another wave takes me down and I'm like a punching bag on a spring, standing up for another, and another, hoping and praying for this brutal pounding to finally come to an end. But I can't pull my feet loose and the frothy white caps and heavy wind tell me I'm in for it, like a wasp trapped in flypaper at the bottom of the sea.

And then I think of her, and with every scorched fiber in what's left of these jellyfish legs I dig deep to draw my right foot from the muck enough to draw it from the sandpit it has burrowed itself into and

I step backward onto something else, I don't know what. It's slick. And sharp. I certainly don't like it. I wildly yank my other foot free of the tar pit below and high step it out of the waist-deep water like a linebacker makes a play down the Astroturf, back to my towel, which has blown several yards down the beach and is now completely covered in sand. I look at it mournfully as I beat the impossible little particles off of it, quickly reminded of my gritty disdain, and I lumber back up to the resort. I can feel the eyes on me. The joggers, the bikers, the afternoon strollers, and beach hikers. I don't dare make eye contact with any of them. Completely demoralized, I decide I'm going to the pool to rinse off.

Children scream as I approach. Not so much at me, as just there are children that are screaming, I think at each other. Taken out of context it sounds like a teenage girl being ax-murdered in a woodshed but in fact, it's a couple of pre-pubescent boys playing tag in the pool. God, I hate screaming. It's even worse than the sand. I can feel the saltwater up my nose and I swear the ear-piercing squeals from that red-headed kid are making it seep into my brain. After a moment I can't take it any longer, this complete ruination of Peace and the continued stifling of my previous positive vibes, so I decide I need to do something about it. Something fun. Something drastic. So, I throw my soiled towel in the dirty bowl bin, strut over to the edge of the pool and do a cannonball right in the middle of them, soaking every single one of the little bastards, as well as their ass-clinched, uppity mommies gossiping on the steps. I apologize the best I can as I climb out of the pool claiming "It was an accident," and "I didn't mean to," and my favorite, "I'm so sorry," all of which are bald-faced lies. Shoot first, ask questions later, bitches. I try not to let my exterior smirk match my internal one as I sashay across the sun deck because the one on the inside is burning a hole in my cheek. I feel great all over again.

I grab three fresh, sunbaked towels from a stack on a table under a folded umbrella, wrap the first around me, and lay the other two on the sun chair. I lie back on the chair, run my hands through my greasy wet hair and take a long look around, sizing up the crowd. Everything in my gut tells me they're sizing up me, too, so I started taking inventory.

My gut's alright. I mean, there's no definition there, but I can suck it in, and I've kept from getting overly fat all these years. There's just zero muscle tone, and I'm horribly pasty. Hopefully, the sun will help. I wonder if I could pass for thirty-five, but there's no way. Maybe forty, at best. So, at least I don't look, you know... *older*. My hands look pretty old though. The skin on them keeps cracking and breaking, folding in tiny lines like the weathered epidermis of a desert lizard. I wonder how old she thinks I am?

My mind races with the possibilities of a new life. I need to prioritize some things. Start making a list. Make a plan. But first, dinner. I remember reading about this chic French restaurant in Lahaina. I wonder if she'll go for that, or if she wants something a little more low-key. No. Girls want to be taken out, treated to a nice meal. They like to be made to feel like they're important. And she *is* important, so why not give her that treat? I wonder how I'll find their number.

And as I lie there absorbing ultraviolet rays from a not-so-distant star I am suddenly shaded, like a looming cloud has blown between me and my only source of energy, and I grow cold.

"Fancy meeting you here."

I open my eyes to see the silhouette of an angel hovering over me, but I am otherwise blinded as I stare into the sun.

"See ya at eight."

I look away, my eyes flush with tears, my retinas scorched from looking directly into the sun, my eyelids drooping over the lenses to relieve the burning sensation across them, and by the time I overcome my temporary moment of blindness, she's gone. I try to regain my focus, regain my energy, regain my full eyesight, but I'm plastered to this molten hot seat and everything I look at has spots.

Where did she go? Did that really just happen, or was that a figment of my imagination?

Did she know I was just thinking about her? But I'm always thinking of her. I wonder if she thinks of me? I imagine our harmonic souls are aligned after taking hallucinogenics together. Or was she just stopping by to pick up her check and take the night off so she can go out with me? Eight o'clock. Eight o'clock. What the fuck am I going to do until eight o'clock?

I sit up, agitated, trying to make sense of it all, still a little bleary-eyed from the sun. I see stars. I feel an uneasy sense of excitement around me. Nervous energy rises up inside of me, making it hard to sit still. The sun beats its heavy rays upon my peeling back and the kids are screaming again, making it harder and harder to concentrate on nothing at all. Maybe it's time for another cannonball.

SKA-DOOOOSH!

* * * * *

I haven't stopped obsessing about her all day. The warm and fuzzy feeling I've been harboring all morning has slowly subsided and been replaced by a slightly nauseating, nervous, excited feeling which I really wish would just go the fuck away. I need confidence. I need a little self-surety. I need a drink. And I also need some pants that don't have two-day old puke on them. I sure get tired of living out of a suitcase.

The carpet is wearing a hole in it where I've paced the better part of the day. From the closet to the bathroom to the window to the minibar, it's a short trip, but I've been weaving an invisible web the past three hours, just waiting for my date to arrive. The TV is of little distraction, repetitiously playing trailers for popular movies available for viewing for a premium sum even I'm unwilling to pay. So, I decide to take a shower. Again. It's my third one today. Thirty minutes later the steam is just clearing out of the bathroom when there's a knock at the door, and I scramble to pull on my shirt.

It's 7:46. Stupidly, I wonder who it could me.

I open the door which immediately hinges on the chain and stops short, cutting my view in half.

It's her, in all white. Like an angel wrapped in a short strappy dress. It's not the most fashion-forward thing I've ever seen, but she looks freaking hot in it. She's got dark smoky eye makeup smeared all around her baby blues and her hair is pulled back off her shoulders in some sort of teased rat's nest, her specialty, which outlines her thin neck revealing a tattoo of a cute little Panda on her right shoulder I hadn't noticed before. She looks completely different than I've ever seen her before. Completely transformed. Borderline Thai Hooker, but I'm not judging. I'm absolutely stunned.

"Hey!"

She also looks nervous. She checks both ways down the hall.

"*Hey.*"

I close the door to take the chain off, then swing it wide open to greet her, completely forgetting I'm not wearing my pants, which are drying on a chair outside.

"Come on in."

She ducks into the room, checking behind her as I close the door.

"If you could just give me a second…"

She's already on the bed, playing on her phone, ignoring me completely. I try to dismiss it as I dry my pants in the bathroom with the hotel hairdryer. They're still damp from where I cleaned the vomit off with soda water from the mini-fridge earlier this afternoon. Sure, it's a little awkward, but it has to be done. It's either that or we could just go ahead and have sex now. I could leave my pants on the rack another twenty minutes or so and they'll be dry and we'll only be fifteen minutes late to dinner. I get a chubby just thinking about it.

She appears in the doorway, adjusting her purse over her shoulder.

"You about ready?"

"Sure." I turn the hairdryer off and put my half wet pants on. "You ever heard of Chez Mer? Everybody says it's the *best*."

"Nope."

"Alright, then. I guess we'll see for ourselves."

We take her car after discreetly walking out the back of the resort to a restaurant next door where she parked. I only think about it after we suspiciously creep through the hallway and down the lit pathways, searching in every direction before deciding on a way to go. I guess she didn't want the Valet to see us together. Or maybe that Samoan Guy that's always working the front desk. But I forget all that as soon as we hop in the car and get on the road. That's when she comes back to me. That smile. Those eyes. Those tits. She's not wearing a bra right now so I am literally staring right at them. Honestly, they're not quite as impressive as I'd hoped, but hey, they're tits. And besides, I don't just like her because of her tits. I like her because-

"Holy Fuck!"

That's me, yelling at the top of my lungs as we careen out of our lane, off the side of the road before correcting into oncoming traffic, and she's screaming at the pick-up truck she passes outside my window-

"WATCH WHERE YOU'RE GOING, ASSHOLE!!!"

Headlights blind us, and I didn't know how deeply religious I was until I started saying Hail Mary's and Jesus Christ's at the top of my lungs, if that does indeed prove any sort of fearful devotion to a higher power of any kind. And just as quickly she whizzes back over into our designated lane, right behind a car going half our speed where she is forced to slam on breaks, almost causing a three-car pile-up with the pickup truck, station wagon and ourselves. But somehow, none of us collide.

"Sweet Virgin Mary Mother of Jesus I'm gonna die."

What *is* it with these Hawaiian people and not being able to drive?

She looks at me with those bunny blue eyes and giggles.

"Calm down. It's just a little traffic."

She slams on the gas and veers into the opposite lane again so she can get around this slowpoke, whom she nods to, before yanking the car back into our lane.

"Sorry. Usually, this road's dead. These assholes are driving so slow"

We come upon two more cars, both of whom are hogging up the right lane and she pauses for only the half-second it takes for the oncoming traffic to whiz past us before she punches it and the whole car takes off, lurching forward as it passes the guy in front of us and the next thing I know we're swinging wide around the second asshole going twenty miles per hour more than him and I get an odd instantaneous compulsion and lean out the window and scream-

"ASSHOOOOOOOOLE!"

94

And God does that feel good. I look over at Mena and she's looking back at me with a glowing expression like I've never been looked at before. My heart leaps out of my tongue and I kiss her, but just as quickly I draw back, utterly humiliated, but she doesn't care. She just keeps driving and smiling and laughing and drifting over the center line on our way towards dinner or death, whichever we're served first.

Fortunately for my appetite, it's dinner, because I'm starving. Although not quite as starving as I was perhaps an hour ago, before the car ride, the butterflies, and the $8 bag of peanuts from the mini-fridge I ate while I was cleaning my pants, of which I ended up having two.

The restaurant is quaint, somebody's old home from way, way back. Not at all what I expected, but perfect, nonetheless. It's a two-story plantation-style home that would be far more fitting in a place like Camden, South Carolina than Lahaina, Hawaii. Poorly maintained but cute as a button, white paint chips off the front porch, and there's a dank musty smell in the hallway which passes through to what looks like an antique museum full of European oak and mahogany. We are wound through modest rooms by the hostess; once dens, living rooms, and bedrooms of the original owners, now small dining rooms with tiny linen-covered tables and elegant place settings, until we arrive on a secluded back patio, overgrown with ivy, and strung with charming rope lights presumably set up for Christmas a few years ago but never taken down judging from the layer of dust and cobwebs that have collected between them. An impressive species of arachnid has made her web not twelve feet away, and it appears she will be dining on a rather large fly at some point during our meal, if not before. Mena doesn't care. I doubt she even notices. The night I've been waiting for all this time is finally here. I order champagne, then wine. Something kind of expensive, but still within reason. Glasses of each. Just enough to make it look like I know what I'm doing. She doesn't know. I doubt she's ever even been to a restaurant like this.

"Is this an oh-seven? Oh-eight was an especially good year." She sticks her nose in it. "Lots of peach. Very acidic." She smiles, approvingly. "Not bad, though."

I nod to the Sommelier and try not to choke on the bubbles. Isn't she full of surprises? I study the menu so I don't fuck anything else up. I'm in deep now. So far, I'm batting a thousand, or five hundred, or whatever that saying is, but you never know. It only takes one mistake to mess everything up. We order oysters, in season, with the Champagne. I figure that will help set the mood. She knows what I'm doing, but she doesn't care. *Pacific Coast Kumamoto's* it reads on the menu. Might as well be French. But it's the best oyster I've ever tasted in my life, with some sort of homemade cocktail sauce we're supposed to mix ourselves, but frankly, the raw shredded horseradish root is so surprisingly tangy and delicious by itself we just eat it raw on the oyster with a miniature three-pronged seafood fork.

Next, are the salads. I have roast pear with blue cheese and walnuts over radicchio, which is a little bitter by itself, but when I eat it all cut and stacked together with the cheese and nuts it's divine. Hers is a traditional Caesar with white anchovies. I'm unimpressed until I taste the anchovy. Salty. Covered in finely shredded Parmesan. My taste buds are delighted. I was adamant I wouldn't try one, but she insisted, and now I'm glad I did. I always heard they were fishy. And hairy. This was just salty. Briny, is what she called it. Delicious, I say. Maybe an old dog can learn new tricks after all?

As the evening heats up, it's only our breath that sours, through oysters and fish and garlic and wine and horseradish. Our palates are alive as we're treated to some of the best food I've ever had, here or anywhere else on earth, and it isn't just her, but a perfect combination of atmosphere and food and wine and company and conversation that culminates into an evening unparalleled and complete. Everything is unimaginably superb. There is no one else I would rather share this with, a night I am unlikely ever to forget.

I have the special, and she has a whitefish in sauce. Broth, really, if I'm going to be exact, which I think is strange, but she keeps raving about fennel and blood orange, so I guess it must be pretty amazing. Sometimes I just need a steak. A man's got to get full. I tell her as much and she rolls her eyes.

"Is that right?" she mocks, giggling.

I'm not quite sure how to take that. Here I am splurging on this ridiculously expensive dinner, of which only 30% can actually be expensed on my travel report due to the expensive bottles of wine and the hefty price tag attached to our Hors d'oeuvres. I can feel myself caving into a void of confusion and self-doubt. I stare at the rare seared meat stuck through the tines of my fork that's been paired with a lovely bottle of Cabernet Sauvignon and think about the cow shit I ate the day before that gave way to an intense introspective insight about my life and where it's headed. Maybe I don't need this. Maybe I don't need any of this, and what I need is to go home and start again. Go home and stop bitching about my life and go out and do something to make it better. Get in shape. Get a dog. Get a life. Work harder. Play harder. Push myself to the limits. Stop fucking about and get outside and Be Somebody for once in my Goddamn life.

"I'm just kidding with you. I love a good steak."

She stabs a bloody piece of flesh from my plate and pops it in her mouth, chewing delightfully, a squinty look in her eye and a red stain on her teeth.

I just stare at her. I don't know how to respond. She stops laughing. I think she's drunk.

"Jeez. You're tense tonight, huh?"

"No. Not at all, actually. Just really, really tired."

"Long night last night, huh?"

"I couldn't sleep when I got home."

"Yeah. Me either."

Kindred spirits.

"Some fucking dog kept barking all night at the house next door. Then a bunch of raccoons got into the trash and we had to pick it up or the landlady who lives across the street will threaten to kick us out again. As if it's our fault the lid won't close all the way."

"Jesus. That sucks. She sounds like a real bitch."

"No... She's okay. I mean, she's right. We did kind of fuck it up."

"Oh."

She looks at me, deep in thought. Her eyes searching me for personal truths I do not have when at last she comes out with it.

97

"No, you're right. She's a bitch."

I grin at her grin, and she grins at me, and then we both look away, both of us unsure of what to do with this undeniable chemistry. I feel it. She feels it. And whenever I just look at her I can't help but skip a breath, or a heartbeat, from the anxiety of my love or lust I don't know, but we're connected, and I just want to scream out *Do You Feel It?* but as I glance at her I know she does even though she's playing with her cell phone again and I grab the nearest waiter over to entice us into dessert, offer us after-dinner drinks, anything to break this unbearable tension and prolong our evening for as long as humanly possible. But then she puts her phone away and I rethink my suggestion. My stomach is killing me, after all.

"I think I'm good, actually."

"Me, too," she says. She looks back into oblivion, and I motion for the check. There's something on her mind tonight. Something lingering in her thoughts, troubling her now, something that she won't quite come out with. And then she's back. A slurp of wine and a wide grin and she says "Well, that was amazing" and the waiter presents the check and our evening resumes.

I leave three hundreds, a couple twenties, a ten and a five and call it quits. She stares at the cobweb hanging over us, with a prolonged look I don't quite recognize. It's not exhaustion. It's not even boredom. There's something inside her, consuming her, yearning to be released. And I am dying to pull the trigger.

"Let's go for a walk." I reach my hand out, fingers motioning for her to follow, and she does, squeaking down the front steps of the old Plantation house like church mice, such an odd place of history on a dark Hawaiian street, and we walk three blocks left until we can see the beach. We jay-walk across the street and within seconds we're kicking off our shoes in the dunes and racing out into the waves.

She kicks water on me and I kick back only I fall down because the water's receded below me and I land in the sand with a splat before a wave breaks in front of us and she grabs my hand and drags me out of the way before I'm hit and it's exhilarating, only now we're wet with sand. We jog out of reach of the water and catch our breath before we mosey down the moonlit beach, arm in arm like the happiest couple on earth.

"That was great" she announces definitively. We're still panting for breath after charging into and out of the ocean, but I try to make conversation. The exercise is nice and all, but it's not why I invited her.

"So... How long have you lived here?"

"On the island?"

"Yeah."

"Couple years."

"Really?"

"Well... I guess it's been like four now. Wow, time goes so fast." She says it like she can hardly believe it.

I can't believe it myself. "Huh."

"Why'd you say it like that?"

"I dunno." I'm not sure how to speak my mind without being offensive, so I just say it. "Just thought you seemed a little more local than that."

"Southern California. Born and raised."

"Oh. Whereabouts?"

"Laguna. Moved down to San Diego for a while for school, but that didn't really work out, so then I came out here... Four years ago, now. Almost five."

"What brought you out here?"

"You're kidding, right?" She looks at me incredulously, as if I'm crazy not to see it. I look around at the Paradise that surrounds me, but it's dark outside. I don't see anything but gray.

"I mean, besides the obvious..."

"Wow. You really want, like, the whole story, huh?"

I shrug. "Just making conversation."

"Well, let's see... I came out here with some girlfriends from college the summer after my sophomore year, and we had the time of our lives. And then about a year later, a couple of us came back."

"Not all of you?"

"No. Laura was just about to graduate, and Nina found a job she really liked and didn't want to leave. My best friend Kylie, she was the one really pushing the whole idea. I guess I didn't have anything better to do."

"And so the two of you moved out here..."

She nods along as I put all the pieces of her puzzle together.

"And you've been here ever since?"

"Yup." She smiles, refreshed to get through the basics.

"What about Kylie? What's she do?"

She gives a nonchalant shrug. "I don't know."

"You don't know?"

"We don't really keep in touch."

"Why not?"

"I dunno. Haven't really talked to her since she moved back to SoCal."

"Oh. What happened?"

She defers. "It's a long story. There was a boy. I don't want to get into it."

"Oh, gotcha... But when she left you weren't ready to go back?"

"Why would anyone want to leave Paradise?"

Those big blueberries gaze up at me as a smirk stretches across her face and we stand there, staring at one another beneath the star-speckled sky.

I'm eager to get back. It's sandy out here. And a bit cold.

"Should we head back?"

She looks around but finds herself in no real hurry. Maybe I should reel it back in. She looks at the ground, moving the sand around with her toe, and then glances back up at me.

"So, what's your deal, anyway?"

"What do you mean?"

I can hear the words before she even says them. "What the hell are you doing here? Don't you have a family? Don't you have someplace to be?"

Work. The *Tournament.* The *Assignment.* My plane leaves tomorrow morning. I haven't written a thing. She has no idea.

But I say none of these things. Instead, she fills the void.

"How long are you planning on sticking around?"

"Not nearly as long as I would like." At least that was honest, however vague.

"Did you ever figure out whatever it is you're running from?"

I smirk, busted. "Not exactly."

"Then how are you ever gonna know what you're running to?"

I search her face for hints of innuendo and validation. All I see is longing. I know it too well.

"I think I'm just gonna go with the flow."

She smiles, comfortably. I've said the right thing.

Her arms wrap around my waist and she leans into my chest as we embrace, awkwardly at first as I search for the right place to put my hands. Her skin is soft against mine, not the leathery lizard skin I've been expecting. And her breath is warm on my arm. The wind picks up and she pulls me closer to her, wrapping me around her like a sweater, and I eagerly oblige. Our damp bodies sandwich together for warmth, only I'm on the outside, the bread to her peanut butter and jelly, a desperate attempt to keep her feelings for me warm. My comfort no longer exists, my body is a shield, hardened and weathered on the outside to protect that which lies underneath, the pearl within my shell. My only sensation comes from the warm spot on my arm and the smell of Pert Plus that wafts my direction from her thin, wispy, over-treated hair. I keep pulling it back to get the strays out of her eyes, and more importantly mine, as the wind whips them around and as I do, she turns, out from under my arm, out from the shield to expose us both to the bittering elements, the warm spot suddenly slipping away from me.

And she kisses me. Not some accidental, excited car kiss devoid of emotion, expression or range, but a *real* kiss. Two-lipped. Full imprint. Our hot breath slowly meeting, her pursed lips like warm silicon pillows, ready for me to rest my own puckered lips upon them. Her jaw parts ever so slowly and I draw her hot sweet breath into mine, tasting the sea salt air and her sea salt lips as I plant my mouth ever more firmly against hers, my neck and hers thrusting our chins together like we're fighting for each other's air, our bodies becoming entangled as our limbs search each other for the right position, the best hold, the most comfortable pretzel that presses our souls as humanly close as possible, grinding against one another until we stick like ice cubes where we're still wet and warm.

And then it's over. She stands back, looking at me, and I at her, a buck mesmerized by her headlights. I want to speak but can't, unable to read her thoughts. I don't want to jeopardize the very slim chance that this will ever go any further. She looks at me with a glint in her eye like she knows exactly what I'm thinking and it's okay because she's thinking it, too, and the only way to transmit these feelings is through her big bunny eyes and pouting lips.

Without a word, she grabs my hand and we're racing. Racing down the beach. Back to her car. Racing down the highway back toward home. Racing to the hotel and into bed. We couldn't have gotten there faster if we'd tried. It wasn't nearly fast enough for me.

We crawl into bed like horny teenagers, kissing, touching, nibbling, giggling, nervously awaiting the moment we know is about to occur, and in this last second quickly and silently decide if it is, in fact, what we really want. The nervousness fades instantly. I take her shirt off as she does mine, then we race to see who can rip each other's clothes off the fastest. It's awkward and clumsy but I easily win.

She pulls me on top of her and as I slip inside our pelvises lock into place as if her small frame were built exclusively for mine, and when she pushes against me I hold strong, giving her something hard and firm to push off against before I thrust back, in a continuous see-saw of guttural grunts and squeals of delight.

She feels incredible, just like I knew she would, ever since that first night at the tiki hut when the cocktail napkin wrapped itself around that cool watery glass and I could see through her shirt. Her fingernails dig into my back like needle nose pliers, pinching up my spine toward the hairline on my neck, which only makes me drive that much harder against her. Our bodies meld into rhythmic harmony as our tribal dance rotates between passages of erotic lovemaking and desperate animalistic humping.

I've never been fucked like this before in my life, and I probably never will be again. I try not to let that depressive thought take up any more room than it already has in my sad weary head as I try to maintain my erection, or the fear that my breath might still reek of garlic and oysters, or the image of a gold-toothed woman chasing me naked around the bedroom with a screaming vacuum, or any other nonsensical image that might draw me away from the task at hand, but to my surprise, despite all these thoughts and many more, they're no distraction at all. I look at her, her tan sagging skin softly rubbing against me, and she closes her eyes. Her lips open and a soft moan escapes her mouth as she concentrates, grinding her hips with sudden direction and purpose against me. She knows what she's doing, and suddenly I wonder how many times she's done this before. Not with tourists. Just sex. She's fucking amazing at it, so I really don't care. I try and tell myself that. We're not protected, but I still feel safe. She wouldn't do anything to hurt me. She's too nice. Besides, it's too late now, so we grind away, impossibly alive after days' worth of sexual tension building up and many years before that of full-on sexual hibernation.

I feel great right now. Alive in so many ways. Only on the internet does sex ever look this good. I had no idea this was even possible, this liberation of self through sex, if that is indeed what is happening. Is this because of her? Or is this feeling just some residual effect of the mushrooms? Or is this a life's worth of sexual fantasizing culminating into the first time ever that the fantasy actually comes true? All because I chose to step off the beaten path, to leap from priority, responsibility, and reason, to take a walk on the wild side, and incidentally, onto a passenger bus loaded full of tourists? Or did this fate begin earlier? When we first met? Upon that very first order? Or when I told her I was on vacation? My very first lie?

"I'm almost there," she gasps.

Are we not there yet? I was jackhammering like a rabbit in heat a while ago, but I'm not even moving anymore. I just lie here, concentrating on the slow rhythm over top of me as every neuron in my entire body fires on all ends. My skin tingles all over. I'm on a mission and I start to grind away again, slowly, measured, and steadfast, perfectly complimenting her heated thrusts. And when it's finally over the sheets are soaked with sweat and my body's sore and she's lying crossways in the bed staring out the sliding glass door exhausted. We take turns going to the bathroom and as I come back to bed I catch her looking at me curiously like she's trying to figure out how old I really am, and if I slipped myself a Viagra or something when she wasn't looking, which would be a compliment considering I've never even used the stuff. What would be the point? When you're home alone with nothing to do, nothing good ever comes from a four-hour boner.

So I lie there and delight in her glow. There's just something about her, like those deep bunny eyes, or that dazed, half-cocked smile, like she knows something important, something that I should know too, and I'll find out when the time's right when she's ready to tell me. I'm not sure exactly what that might be, but something keeps drawing me in. She puts my t-shirt on as she tiptoes into the bathroom. I take a sip of water, cleansing my palate one last time, and check the clock to see how many more hours I can shirk off before I need to start packing for my flight.

My flight… Oh my God… Am I still going on my flight? It's almost 2 a.m., but I'm not the least bit tired. Energized is more like it. Rearing to go. I hear the toilet flush and she exits the bathroom, unsure of where to go and what to do.

I reach out to her, and she strides over. I pull her toward me, and she amuses me despite her obvious growing fatigue. And so I kiss her. Like in the car. On the beach. Right on the lips. And I don't stop.

She turns her cheek. "What's gotten into you?"

"You."

I keep kissing her, but she's a wet fish, gone to sleep. She falls into bed beside me and I scoot over to give her the spot I was in, the spot she's already taken, and I cover her with the soft sandy sheet.

She peeks over it, timidly.

"You're not going to leave me, are you?"

She must know about the flight. I never told her but she knows. Everyone knows everything about everybody around here.

"Of course not. How could I?"

I smile at her, and she looks deep within me. Deeper than anyone's ever looked before, searching for answers I feel certain my glazed red eyes can't answer. Or maybe I already did. She pulls me against her, squeezing every inch of body she has against mine, wrapping me up like a blanket, pulling me over her face and taking my

104

breath out from under me until I almost forget where I am. I'm rock hard again, and could just as easily start this all over again, and I want to, but something's telling me no. So we lie there embraced in each other's arms as we try to sleep.

"I'm gonna miss you."

"I'm gonna miss you, too."

I immediately regret saying it. It's like I just confirmed her darkest fears, that I really *am* going to leave her, and *this* right here... *This* is it. *This* is all she's good for, and now, now that this is done, I'm going home.

There's noticeable quiet. I don't know what else to say, so I say nothing. Even worse.

We lie side by side in bed, staring at the ceiling, minds racing, without a word across our lips. My mind is reeling, I could talk all night, but there's something on her mind that I want to know, but can't afford to ask. I don't want to ruin another moment, so I wait for her to say it.

"What do you want to be when you grow up?"

"Seriously?"

"Seriously."

That's not exactly what I had in mind, but it'll do. I don't think twice.

"A science-fiction novelist."

"Seriously?" I can hear the disdain in her voice.

"Seriously."

"Weak sauce." She stares at the ceiling, deep in thought.

"What about you?" I can't wait to unlock the infinite mysteries from her mind.

She ponders it for some time, looking up into the dark white ceiling as if it holds all the answers in the world, then nudges her head into her pillow and closes her eyes. And with deep sincerity and thought she finally reveals it, her deepest darkest passion.

"An astronaut." And she turns over and goes to sleep.

5
Thursday

I barely sleep at all. All I can keep thinking is *Astronaut? Really? What the fuck is that?* I had so much more to say if she was willing to talk, but she rolled over and that was it. Maybe that was it, I dunno. Maybe it wasn't. Maybe it was only it because after she rolled over I didn't do anything else. I didn't pursue it anymore. I got what I wanted and she got what she wanted and that was that. Only we didn't, I don't think. Not now that I look back on it, anyway. There were things I wanted... Questions answered, emotions reciprocated, the feeling of togetherness that was so strong between us for that hour, or for those few hours... I wanted that longer than we had it. I don't know. Maybe we did have that. Maybe we still do.

After fifteen minutes of lying there, I could hear her breathing deepen. She seemed asleep. I was pretty sure she was. I was still awake, just thinking about our night. That incredible, mind-numbing, pelvis bruising sex. My mind raced: *Was that good enough? Is that what she wants? Can I really make her happy? Do I even want to?*

And the answer, to my surprise, was a resounding and overwhelmingly emphatic yes. That was exactly what I wanted. *Paradise.* To live under the moon, on the sand, with the stars and this angelic brown beauty with the bunny eyes and blonde hair and a button nose who has rescued me from the very demons that sent me here. Work. Assignments. Responsibilities. These are the things I loathe and detest, the irrepressible obstinacies of society, the scourges of life that betray us our ability to ever truly be free, that deny us the real liberty of the pursuit of happiness, all because we are trapped on a never-ending hamster wheel of death. But here, in Paradise, I can escape all of that. I can escape everything. I can even escape reality, it's only a cow patty away. And it's magnificent here. I want her. I want to be with her. I want to consume her, like last night, but even more, so that we can become spiritually one and for us to live like a tree on the beach forever bearing fruit into existence from our great and powerful loins, and feeding the village with our knowledge as we tan and wrinkle and age forever until the end of time, like two dates melting into sugar in the drowsy heat. I can feel the warmth of the sun upon my leaves. I can hear the lapping of the waves against the unrelenting sand, and some children squealing with delight as they play beneath my shade.

Children. I've never even wanted children before. I've despised them until now. But now I picture it, an entire idyllic future laid out before me, and by my side, the woman who made it all possible. Mena.

And now here I am. Lying here. In the middle of the morning. In love. In lust. Shared bliss. Perpetual harmony. Ready to tie the knot and run away with this woman to the end of the world, which couldn't be that far away considering our remote location to begin with. We are ready to intertwine our branches and our belongings and our lives from here on out, together. Here we are. In love.

But when I wake up, she's gone. I don't think much of it at first. I pull the sheet over me, and when the weight of her leg, which had held it down seemingly only moments before is gone and the sheet draws easily, I sit up.

"Mena?"

I think this is the first time I've ever called her by her name. But no one comes. No one answers.

I check the bathroom. Empty. Sitting room, empty. I throw on a shirt and walk out the open glass sliding door with the hope she's out back, sipping coffee in a robe, or my t-shirt, or reading the daily paper that's left at the door every morning, planning the rest of our day, from the meals we'll eat to the sights we'll see, and everything in between.

But she's not there. The wind is really whipping, and I bring in an inflatable pool toy that's blown my way. I slide the glass door closed, drop the toy on the floor and sit on the edge of the bed, staring at it, thinking. *What to do? What to do?*

My flight is supposed to leave soon, but I can't leave now. I'm expected to get back tonight and turn in my final draft tomorrow, but for what? A lousy thousand bucks? If I'm lucky? Despite my ridiculous bar tab, dinner, and the raid on the mini-fridge, I really haven't racked up that much of a tab. Then I quickly realize I'll have to turn in something, some kind of paper at least mentioning the freaking tournament or they'll make me reimburse them for everything, the flights, hotels, everything, even though they get some kind of ridiculous corporate discount because they send people out here all the time. If I don't turn in anything, they'll hit me with the full retail fare just to recoup some of their loss, the bastards. I know how this works. So, I have to turn in *something*, but what that is, or what that will look like is currently completely up for debate. I've got less than 36 hours to figure it out. Oh well, if they want *my* take on the tournament, that's exactly what they're going to get. Right now, it's the only thing I've got.

My alarm clock goes off. It's 7:05. Time to get up and catch that plane. Only I'm not going anywhere.

I run the water in the shower for a long time before I finally get in. I find myself staring at my aged skin in the mirror, at this brittle, wrinkled skin around my eyes, and the dark puddles of sagging skin below, until the mirror is so foggy I can no longer see my father's reflection, and I open the glass shower door and step inside, letting the warmth of the water and the steam consume me. I take a few deep breaths before I put my face on the cool part of the tile again, not near as cool today thanks to the fiery hot shower scalding me from the spigot above. I hold on to the wall as visions of last night blur through me. Saliva. Moaning. Soft lips. Sweat. Convulsions. I remember it all in one quick mental montage and I can feel the blood surge through my brain and I gasp for breath, but the only air I have to breathe is hot and suffocating as the boiling hot water sears the back of my head. My body numb, I start to waver when I plant my entire self against the cool marble wall. I tremble from the heat and from the fear that after last night I might never see Mena again and I try to catch my breath and relax. Of course, she isn't *gone* gone. She just left. She's got work to do or something. Probably just went home to sleep. Feed her dog, or goldfish, or whatever. There are a million reasons why she wouldn't stay 'til morning. Why do I always have to second guess things all the time? But then again, why didn't she say goodbye?

The blood seeps slowly out of my head and gradually rejuvenates the rest of my body so that my brain can function adequately enough to switch the water off and get out of this suffocating shower. Steam pours out as the door swings open, fogging up all the glass mirrors and tile floors even more than they already were. My head spins, but I try to stay focused as I dry myself off and walk to the other room, butt ass naked. All the curtains are drawn, but I don't care. Nobody's interested in me, and I'm only interested in one thing: seeing Mena again. And suddenly, all the hopes and fears and anxieties I've been harboring about work and about life and about love, they slip away and I realize everything will be okay. The world is different now. *I'm* different. I'm making decisions for myself again. I'm the master of my own domain. And I'm ready to take on this new life that awaits me, whatever that entails. Nothing can bring me down.

I put my clothes on, one pant leg at a time, not quite as casual as yesterday, but I'm not in a suit either. The suit's ruined, who am I kidding? But these linen slacks are comfortable, and I roll up the sleeves to my untucked button-down shirt to give it a cooler Hawaiian vibe. I slide on my docksiders and the transformation is complete. I finally look and feel like I belong somewhere. Right here in Paradise. Right where I am.

I stroll down the hallway, superficially confident that I've got the world on a string. I enter the resort restaurant expecting to be surrounded by pen pushers and hair gel experts, big foam finger-wavers and adults who paint letters on their body to help support student-athletes, and old people milling about the coffee station or trying to figure out the toaster oven. Instead, there's none of that. Just me. Me and a couple of Japanese women enjoying their Belgian waffles in silence. And quite a few members of the serving staff rearranging the tables into a large buffet against the wall. I make myself a cup of coffee and sit down, enjoying my view of the outside gardens. Halfway through my cup, I consider that before I do anything else I should probably tell the hotel I'm not checking out so they don't assume I'm leaving and void my key. Keep them from doing whatever it is they do with stuff that's left behind. Sell it in the gift store. Put it in the lost and found. Or do they just take it for themselves?

I stride up to the front desk like a man without a care in the world, but when I get to the reception area I can barely get through. Everybody in the hotel is here. All of the hair teasers and teeth bleachers and high school champions and octogenarian diaper wearer's and, incredibly, now that I'm standing here with all of them up close and personal, intermingling within this salad bowl of diversity, I actually realize something: they all look a lot like regular people. People I can identify with. People I'd hang out with. I wouldn't have even recognized them if I hadn't already seen them in their natural habitat, made up in eyeshadow or jersey material or tourist hats and knee-high socks, either at the game, or at the conference, or milling about the gift shop in search of the perfect keepsake. I squeeze through the crowd to assimilate into what I best discern is the line that leads to the desk and patiently wait my turn.

My mind races with opportunism about all the wild adventures I might parlay into astonishing fables in such a place. Like Hemingway in Paris, or even better, the Caribbean, this place will be the hub from which all inspiration is born, for what is sure to become my Era of Greatness as I create the masterpiece of my catalog. With all the intricacies of Hawaiian lingo, customs, and behavior permeating my nascent style and informing a point of view that has until now been missing from narrative fiction--

"Aloha. Are you checking out?"

His voice almost catches me off guard. How long have I been standing here? I step up to the desk where Bill, the Samoan concierge in a bright floral print shirt, greets me with an engaging smile. He has long black hair pulled back in french braids with orchids decorated throughout that match the blue orchid lei around his neck. He looks like this every day, coordinating the flowers in his hair with the ones in his shirt, which takes quite a lot of devotion and planning, for him and his florist.

"No, actually, I'd like to extend my stay."

"Fell in love with the place, did you?"

I can see right through his passive aggression.

"I guess so."

"And what room are you in?"

"Number 1352."

As if he doesn't know. He types something into his keyboard before he comes back with

"Mr. Shaw?"

"That's correct."

He types something else in his keyboard. I'm starting to get paranoid. What all could he be typing in that thing?

Warning: guest has a tendency to fall in love with resort staff, please keep any and all single females away from him. Maybe all females. Maybe everyone. Maybe we should make him take care of himself. Maybe we shouldn't let him stay here at all!

"Okay. And for how many days would you like to stay?"

It's a good question. One I somehow hadn't anticipated him asking. I give it pause for thought.

"Mmmm... Indefinitely."

"Oh. I *see*." The judgment in his expression is much clearer now. I'd be a fool to miss it.

This could get expensive, I consider. And I probably won't get that corporate rate. This will all be on my own dime. I've got to finish that article. And the thousand or so bucks I'm getting for that won't get me far.

"Probably only for a couple of nights. We'll see."

"Playing it by ear, are we? Just sorta... winging it?"

This guy. I can smell the disgust in his mouth, and it smells like Altoids, and like Altoids, it is curiously strong.

"Guess so."

I pat the counter like we've wrapped up and walk off.

"Sir..."

I act like I don't hear him and the eager beaver behind me jumps up to bat and the Samoan is left with a few unanswered questions of his own. Like who's paying for this room. I'll settle up in a couple days. It's not like I don't already have a credit card on file.

I swoop through the crowd, ready for action, ready for anything really, except what I get.

"Frank!"

Oh no. I act like I don't hear him. It worked the last time.

"Franky baby! What's happenin' man?"

I stop. There's no way out of this. I turn, and sure enough, there's Eddie... uhh, Eddie what's his name, and he's grinning ear to ear.

"Where the hell ya been? I haven't seen you all week! I knew you'd be here, you old bastard, but you weren't in the press room. And you weren't in the locker room. And you didn't come to opening night, surprise surprise... Oh! But you know where I did see you...?"

I can't wait.

"Was that you roaming around the floor with the photographers the other day? Checking out all the cheerleaders on the floor?" He punches me in the arm. *Hard.* "You dirty dog! I knew that was you, you ol' sunuvabitch!" He slaps me on the shoulder like a proud father to his son. "How ya been?"

"Good." I downplay it.

"How 'bout that game, huh?"

And before I know it, he's droning on about numbers and scorecards, and players and coaches and name dropping people like I should know who he's talking about but I'm just getting more and more confused and all I want is to order a Bloody Mary with a peel and eat shrimp and a celery stalk and dump it on his head.

"What are you doing here? You staying at this dump? We're over at the Sheraton Black Rock and let me tell you something, that place is amazing... They do this show right out over the water, you'd love it. And the sea turtles... You can practically ride 'em! I did! I couldn't believe it! And the buffet, Oh... They got salmon, and this mushroom thing, omelets, quiche... literally, eggs any way you want 'em. And that's just for breakfast. You should see the fuckin' spread they got for dinner!"

He looks around, sizing the place up. "But I mean, yeah, this place is nice. I can see why you'd want to stay here. It's quaint, huh? Nice and *quiet*."

I can't stand to hear the sound of his voice right now. All I want is a little peace, a little solace to sit and think and figure out my next move, be it another trip to the beach, *doubtful*, or the pool, or the bar, or on a cab ride around the island, searching for her house, or something more drastic, something more dangerous entailing me in a high-speed chase on a motorcycle, back down the treacherous Road to Hana. Only this time, I'm not chasing spiritual enlightenment, I'm chasing love. A love that neither of us can deny, and that I will not let her run from. I get it now. She's afraid, and I am too. These feelings, they came on so strong, so fast, but I know everything will be okay. For the first time in a long time I have a warm feeling in my gut that this moment of separation, these agonizing minutes away from one another are but a temporary misunderstanding in our ever-evolving vocabulary of love, and if only we can share another passing glimpse then she will know my love for her and no longer feel the need to run away. And we will finally be together as we are in my imagination. In my dreams.

"You know who else is staying here? Larry Epson."

I have no idea who that is, but the way Eddie's ogling me I get the feeling I should.

"No kidding."

"You seen him?"

I shake my head and look away as if I could spot him any moment, this mystery man whom I've never met. Eddie mistakes this as an invitation to keep on yapping about the intricacies of the tournament we just witnessed, as if I was there, as if I ever gave two shits to begin with. This player did this. This coach did that. This team flamed out early. This one was a surprising dark horse, but they couldn't quite pull it off in the end. Yadda yadda yadda.

I swear, I really am trying to listen, for my own personal gain, of course, hoping I can retrieve a tidbit here or a factoid there, maybe even a couple of stats I can throw out in order to make it sound like I really know what I'm talking about in this article I'm never gonna write, but in the end, it's all gibberish to me. He might as well be speaking Italian.

I met Eddie at one of these types of events years ago, I don't remember which, and now it's like every assignment, there he is. Somehow we've gotten picked up by the same lousy b-level press circuit- either up-and-coming or flaming-out publications that are scrambling to get their foot in the door with a very fickle and eternally evasive audience. So basically, they just throw shit at the wall to see what color sticks. Eddie's the type that's always got something to complain about. You know the ones. The hotel's never clean enough, or there weren't enough towels, or the stipend barely covers anything, didn't get a good seat at the game, everybody around him is an idiot… blah, blah, blah.

I survey the room using all the body language I know to communicate to Eddie I'm over this conversation and ready to go on with my day, but he doesn't get it. He doesn't get a lot of things. He just keeps rambling on about fucking Larry what's-his-face and side-eyeing every remotely cute woman from the business conference in a tight shirt and velour pants that passes. He is truly pathetic. I cut him off mid-exchange and abruptly exit the lobby, leaving Eddie there alone, surrounded by dozens of other people he can talk to that aren't me.

I walk outside to get some fresh air as the sun peaks through the morning clouds, and I hear the gentle cry of a blissful child, splashing in the water. I round the ornate planters past the tiki hut where I see him: a beautiful little boy, squealing with delight on the side of the pool as he jumps in, turning midair, and catching himself on the wall, before shimmying carefully over to the ladder and climbing back out, repeating the process again and again with a growing excitement and confidence with each and every mid-air turn.

These are the actions of a child who so desperately wants to grow up, to do something he is not allowed or not yet able to do, that he has devised his very own game to satiate that intrinsic desire to get wet, to submerge ourselves and swim, so that we can return to the blissful warmth of the womb.

He can't be more than four. Maybe he's five, I dunno. I was never good at those things. He pauses as he gets out of the pool and stares at me, as I stare back at him, and I think about a wide-open future with endless possibilities, for him and me, and I decide to sit down, get a little sun, and enjoy the day.

It's a beautiful pool, I don't know why I haven't spent more time here this past week. The sun's shining gloriously by now, and I bring the back of the lounge chair up a notch so I can sit up to watch the boy who continues his circuit inside the pool.

Like a wind-up toy, he does the same thing again and again, like clockwork. I get the feeling the kid would stop if his mom would only look at him after his repeated ignored attempts to get her to. But alas, he's doomed to go on in this failed attention deprived loop forever. Or at least as long as she's on her cell phone.

"Mom! Look!" he says, as he jumps in, twists, grabs the wall, and splashes the side of the hard-tiled edge with a tiny scream of glee. I admire him from afar. His slight little body. His wild-eyed grin. The kind of grin only a jubilant little kid without a worry in the world could have. Without fear of consequence or retribution, without fear of bigotry or condemnation. Without fear of life, or death, or sickness, or pain, or anything at all. All he knows is the perfect bubble of happiness that surrounds him in his infinitely curious and wonderful mind. Beautiful on the inside, as well as the out, for he is pure. Pure joy. Pure beauty. A pure life. A pure state of being. Before the decrepit influence of age and society beats against you like the water beats the volcanic rock and pounds you into sand.

Each time the little boy rises from the ladder, pockets of water drain from his swim shorts, pitter-pattering against the concrete surface that he skitters over before springing back in the pool. Splash! He pulls himself up again, his swimsuit full of water again spilling all over the outside of the pool. Slippery feet splish-splash through it before he leaps off the edge, closer and closer to the end of the pavement each time, before he spins, grabs, and goes under, re-surfacing again and again.

Water accumulates into a small stream as the little boy's bathing suit continues to scoop it from the pool. And he runs through it, toes leaping from the last possible millimeter of concrete before hanging in the air, turning mid-jump, facing the wall, and grabbing hold of the wall on his way down with such pride! Oh, what a kid! What a cute, and innocent, and splendid young being full of hope and wonder and imagination, whose smooth mind has concocted this silly game with utmost excitement where he finds total contentment in the repeated actions therein. No distractions. No deviations. Just this.

What a marvelous, sensational boy. To have such a boy of my own would be a blessing. A joy as pure as the love he was born out of. And his parents would love him to no end, as they love each other and themselves, so that he can be raised in a protected and nurturing environment where he will never face hunger, or pain, or disappointment or disillusionment or disdain or anything on this earth that could harm him because he is a product of purity and light. And we would be the best parents we could possibly be, showering our children wholeheartedly with the attention they deserve instead of sitting there, jabbering on our cell phone ignoring the Joyous Life before us.

Splash!

Chlorine-filled water drips over the concrete as his tiny feet race in a tight semi-circle. Slick toes vault from the slippery surface into the air, and he turns, so completely, so perfect in his form, and his smile, from ear to ear, screaming with glee as his toes hit the water and his hands grab the concrete and he--

Smack—

His chin, a mere centimeter over the line, cracks against the concrete siding with unbridled pain and agony rattling through the child's head and neck—

He goes under. The muffled squeals of a four-year-old bubble under the surface and the mom tosses her phone and dives in the water and collects him like a drowned baby from a giant bathtub as he writhes, sopping and bloodied against her.

I stand up, for what reason I am not sure. To help? But I am of no help, as I am in more shock than any save the boy. To watch? Possibly, though my view before was just as clear, of the spot on the pavement, where his tiny chin left a sliver of blood, and of the water, murky and polluted, like an octopus squirted a cloud of maroon ink that slowly dissipates into the rest of the pool, turning the aqua blue into a steely cool gray. The boy lies on the sun deck gushing blood down his neck and chin like his throat has been slit, just waiting to die as his jugular empties out onto the patio. His mother is by his side, holding a towel against him, calm in her actions as the boy shakes in fear below. She wipes his forehead with another towel as she directs the waiter for some water. A mother is prepared at all times. A mother is someone who knows how to handle each and every situation as they arise, calmly and sensibly. They are boy scouts with vaginas, and the white towels pile up like soiled maxi pads beside her. The boy will be fine, but I might not.

Suddenly I realize why I'm standing. It is to flee. I am not cut out for this. The mere thought of blood makes me squeamish, and to see this poor innocent boy, once smiling with the grace of an angel, now lying here with a gash in his chin the size of the Mariana Trench, still gushing with blood like a pig waiting to be buried in a spit, makes me feel like I'm going to vomit all over again.

So much for fresh air, I think to myself when a sudden urgency washes over me. I'm just wasting my time. Right here and now, but also before. A whole life wasted, as long as she's not in it. What have I been doing all this time? Just sitting around, watching the days roll by? Rubbernecking at other people's train wrecks along the highway to hell? Well, I'm making a decision and I'm not sitting by idly anymore. I need to find her. I need to find out why she didn't say goodbye to me and tell her how I feel. I need to confirm what I already know. I need to know she feels it, too. What we shared last night was something two people only get once in their whole life, and I'm not gonna let it pass me by. And I can't wait until six o'clock, or whatever time her shift usually starts at the tiki. I need to find someone around here who can tell me where I can find her now.

I circle over the bridge to the tiki hut, but she's not there, of course, so I meander back inside. I wander through the restaurant just to see if I can find anyone, the server I asked before, perhaps? The place is slowly filling up with guests. It's lunchtime and they've got a special going for Thanksgiving. I spot the manager chatting up a table of happy diners by the turkey carving station and make my way over.

Wait, is it Thanksgiving already? I can't believe it, almost another year is passed, and this is all I have left to show for it. My heart hardens and I pause, unsure of what to do next. He's right there, and he knows where to find her. I know he can help. I just have to ask him. This is my only chance. For love and for happiness. I bite my lip and put my best foot forward and step right up to him.

"Excuse me."

"Yes?"

"Can you tell me where I can find Mena?"

He gawks at me. I might as well have told him I was pregnant. "She's kinda short, blonde hair, real tan…"

He cuts me off, sternly. "Yeah, I know who she is, but that's no business of yours."

I wonder if I've offended him in some way like he has his own vested interest in the girl and I'm on his turf now.

"I just wanted to thank her. For a job well done."

"It's company policy not to give out the personal information of our employees to anyone, including, and especially, our guests."

He looks at me squarely.

"And if your interest is to fraternize with employees at our resort, perhaps you'll find another hotel more accommodating."

A grease fire suddenly erupts in the kitchen and he is forced to storm off and handle it, pushing the chefs away just in time before they dump water all over it. He grabs a towel and whips the flames with it until they eventually die out, suffocating their ability to spread and consume anything else in their path. Deprived of all air, the flames are extinguished, leaving nothing on the stovetop but char and ash.

The fire is contained. But not my hopes of finding information. I am a man unhinged, and I plot my next move with great urgency. I head to the bar, hoping to find a recognizable face. That older chick from the Tiki hut, or maybe Ken. Hopefully not Ken. But then again, at this point, I'll take what I can get. I'll take the lady with the gold tooth if she doesn't suck me into her vacuum. Anybody who might know something about Mena, I've got about fourteen hundred dollars or so of cash left in my stipend, and I'm willing to spend every dime if it leads me to her. There's so much to say. So much to know. So much to get ready and figure out before I take off, and I can't wait any longer.

Fuck. It's Ken. He mixes Bloody Mary's and fills trays of champagne glasses with orange juice and bubbly from behind the bar. I think twice about approaching him but I'm already this deep so I might as well dive all the way in.

"Hey man," I offer as I pony up to the bar.

He looks tired. Distant. Like he's just going through the motions. Maybe he was up all night fucking some hot chick, too. He looks at me from a distant lens with a heavy daze, almost smiling, but when he realizes it's me I swear he scowls.

And *then* he smiles. That bright and cheery Hawaiian smile.

"Aloha!"

"Aloha."

I don't know if he's saying hello or goodbye, but I can take a guess. I sit down at the bar anyway.

"Hail Mary?" He sets something on the bar in front of me, as if he'd been waiting on me this whole time. It's hot pink, mostly, with loads of pepper and spices floating inside, with a Shrimp, Olive and piece of celery sticking out of it, and a heavily salted rim."

"Excuse me?"

"It's my own invention. Usually, a Hail Mary's a virgin Bloody Mary, but who the hell wants that? So I double the vodka and add a spoonful of Greek yogurt to help tone it down."

"That sounds absolutely disgusting."

"People tell me they love it. Of course, they could just be saying that. Sometimes people have a hard time deciphering what's good or bad, smart or stupid…"

He eyes me with a wide grin.

"Appropriate and inappropriate… You know?"

He laughs to himself as he starts polishing the next batch of champagne glassware. It's a jolly old laugh, warm and inviting. If only he wasn't laughing at me.

"People are so dumb."

I glare at him with my best smile, and, to get his attention, grab the Hail Mary and toss some back.

Just as I suspected, it's the worst thing I've ever tasted in my entire life. I gag, wanting to spit it out, but I somehow manage to push it down my hollow throat as quickly as I know how in hopes that it will not come right back up.

"Well, at least you gave it a shot. That's what it's all about." He dumps the drink and offers me a menu. "So, what can I set you up with?"

Before I can answer, he lays his cards bare.

"And don't you dare mention her name."

"Excuse me?"

"Don't act like you don't know. Don't even play that."

"Ken…"

"No."

And I'm suddenly struck with the realization that not only was our secret little rendezvous not a secret, but the whole hotel knows. I'm sure it doesn't help that I keep asking perfect strangers that work here about her.

More alarming, however, is my concern about how much he might know.

"How much do you know?"

"Enough."

I taunt him. It's the only tool at my disposal.

"Like *what*?"

"I know she had to carry you home the other night you were so God damned drunk after you must have told her how pretty her eyes were about four dozen times."

I *did?*

"And last night she called out sick and it's the first night all week you haven't been posted up at seat three like you're paying rent, only to hear the two of you were seen scurrying in the back exit about one a.m. and she hasn't been seen since. And here you are, sitting at my bar, with the gall to ask me about her. That's what I know."

A ticket prints on a small computer behind him and he rips it off, quickly pouring a mimosa before setting it at the server pick-up station. He tries to avoid me, but it's impossible with me at the center of his bar. I wait until he's right in front of me to corner him.

"Hear me out, at least."

"It's time for you to go."

"What did I do?"

"You know what you did."

"I need to see her."

"I said no!"

Ken is livid. I've never seen a natural-born Hawaiian so aggravated before.

"You people always think you can just come here on your spring break, or your family vacation, or whatever the fuck, and you can just act however you want, do whatever you want to do, however indecent, with no regard for those who literally spend their lives serving you. Then you just go back to your expensive homes on the mainland, back to your nice jobs and your perfect families, and you don't care. Why would you? You only care about yourselves."

I've heard those words before. A little over six years ago. Right before she walked out the door.

Only this time he's wrong. I do care about others. One other in particular, who I want to love and nurture and protect for the rest of my life so that we can stay together always, starting as soon as I can get some information on how to track her down.

"Please... Ken... It's my only chance. It's important."

Ken looks off. He can't stand there forever.

"Anything you can give me. A number. An address. Anything."

He scowls at me. A wave of fury crashes over him and he hurls his towel at the sink in defeat before storming over to the check printer. He presses a button and a slip of paper shoots out, which he rips off before checking an app on his phone. He scribbles something down on the paper, wads it up and turns around facing me squarely across the bar. He's definitely scowling now. I can hear his engine growl.

"What are you gonna do, huh? When you find her? What are you gonna say?"

"I-"

"There's nothing you can say."

He glares at me with daggers shooting from his eyes and throws the piece of paper at me.

"Do what you gotta do, then get off my island, you fucking prick." And with that, he rips the towel from the sink and marches down the bar.

I slide backward off the stool and lean over to pick the wadded piece of paper from off the floor. I quickly uncrumple it, just to see what treasures it might behold and find an address. An address I don't recognize. *Her address.*

"Thanks." I smile at Ken. He smirks back, and there's genuine happiness in there somewhere, I know it. Maybe he knows I'm different. Maybe he knows I'm going to do the right thing. I mean, aren't I? What even is "The Right Thing?" I'm going back to see her, one last time. To discuss the future. To discuss the past. Maybe when I kiss her goodbye I can take her one last time real quick before I go, to remind her how much I care for her so she won't cheat on me while I'm away, and then maybe in a month or so, around Christmas, I'll fly back out and see her again. But for longer next time. Maybe I'll stay for two weeks instead of one. Or maybe even longer, who's to say? I've got nothing tying me down to the mainland. No home. No life. Maybe I'll do what she did and just stay here. Come out, visit, fall in love. I mean, look at this place, it's absolutely stunning. It's the Garden of Eden. A heavenly dream come true. It really is Paradise.

I'm in love and on the move and in a taxi now, except instead of pulling right, out into the flood of escorts driving their patrons to the nearby pineapple airport where they'll take off back to their homes on the mainland, back to their 9 to 5's and bitter wives and to the same redundant life that makes heart disease the leading cause of death outside commuter car accidents, we go left, northwest on the highway, up to a part of the island that I, and most other tourists I would imagine, have never been.

It's not long before we pull in. We take a right off the main road, and then a quick left. There are some low scruffy palm trees, thick with dead palm fronds, not the clean, pretty, manicured kind they have at the resort. And there's little if any grass. Just small patches here and there where it peeks out between the rock and dirt. Some remnants of gravel form a road to nowhere, half-paved forty plus years ago, abandoned, and long since forgotten. Now it's a makeshift cul-de-sac. Not much to look at. A couple of low lying shotgun houses, shacks really, with screened-in porches, and paint chipped siding. Most of the screens blow loosely in the breeze. There are six houses total, if you can call them that, all around the cul–de-sac, which look like they were built on two lots. They all share a driveway, the gravel road, but they're separate homes, with separate mailboxes and separate families divided amongst them. The address on the receipt paper is for the first one on the left. Mena's house, or so I'm hoping. I wonder what makes a girl who probably clears several hundred a night want to live in such a dilapidated corner, but quickly brighten to the idea that she doesn't need glitz and glamour to be happy. Just a roof over her head and a quiet view of the water, which looks serene from here, down the hill, beneath the cliffs. The resorts line the coastline to the left, each with its own sprawling entryway and impeccable landscaping. You can see a lot from up here, surprisingly. An old lady sits in a tattered lawn chair to my right admiring the same view as me. Could be a relative. Probably not. Maybe the landlord. Who knows.

I get out of the taxi, nervously, unsure whether to keep him around or pay him to leave. I decide to pay him. This might take a while. I wipe my greasy palms on my pants, take a long calming breath, and ring the doorbell. Nothing happens, so I firmly knock.

Within two seconds the inside door swings wide open-

"Hello?"

A stocky looking punk stands before me. I faintly recognize him, I think, but I'm too caught off guard by the sound of a crying baby and another kid, a girl, maybe three, screaming inside.

"Daddy! Make him stop!"

I look at the address on the paper again, and it hits me: This isn't the right address. Ken punked me, that bastard.

"You want somethin'?" This guy looks agitated. Maybe it's the handful of kids he's got to take care of, but his tone is terse, and I don't feel the need to keep him any longer than I have to.

"I'm sorry to bother you. I was looking for somebody, but I think I've got the wrong house." That double-crossing bastard. Probably knows this guy's an ass-whoopin' motherfucker just waiting for people to knock on his door, like Mormons, or Jehovah's Witnesses, or those people that stop by to literally sell you shit. You know what I'm talking about, the ones with the manure they want to sprinkle on your lawn, then charge you for it? But I can smell what they're up to. And now I'm pissed. I swear, I drove all the way out here, wasted thirty dollars on a damn cab ride which isn't even around anymore just to look like a friggin' idiot in front of this freaking guy. How am I gonna get back now?

"You lookin' for Mena?"

I can't believe it. This is the place. I perk up.

"Yeah. You know where she is?"

Maybe Ken wasn't dicking me around after all! He really *does* want me to make things right. That's best for everyone, right? I mean, who wouldn't want that?

"You've got some fuckin' nerve."

Before I know what's happening the screen door is pushing me outward and then it's his fists against my head and my cheeks battering me to the ground. My right eye catches a blow or two, my eyebrow, my ear, my shoulder, my arm; I'm ducking and turning, trying to escape any way I can but I can't tear away fast enough. He reaches in and pulls me apart like a soft doughy pretzel, picking me to pieces before grabbing me by my collar and standing me back up straight and catching me with a quick uppercut to the gut followed by a jaw-cracking right hook to the side of my face. I drop to the ground like a shelf full of books, hard and all over the place.

"I don't ever want to see you on this island again. You understand?"

I don't know who this guy is or why he doesn't like me or what I could have possibly done in the thirteen-point-five seconds I had on my feet before he hit me to deserve any of this, so I nod the best I can and listen as his boots march back across the loose gravel and the screen door slams shut. That's all I can do, is listen. Everything else aches. My palms and my face burn like scalded meat, my insides are bruised to the marrow of my core. I pry myself off the gravel driveway and sit up, picking the loose stones from my delicate hands. Everything bleeds. My nose. My mouth. My head. My pride. I even busted my kneecap open on a rock when I fell. There's blood dripping all over my nice linen pants. Shit. My temple is slit from where I caught a blow to the face, and worst of all my nose is probably broken. I touch it and wince; it's definitely broken. I look up to find the Ass Whooper's kids ages one and three standing at the screened-in door, watching through the mesh as Daddy's latest conquest picks himself off the ground.

I look at them. At their soft, blue bunny eyes, their long straight blonde hair, their overly tan little bodies, and suddenly, I get it. I know who they are. I understand this whole situation now. And I feel ridiculous. This feeling in my gut, and in my jaw, against my teeth, and in my ribs, at least one of which is certainly to be cracked, suddenly throbs even worse, overtly magnified by my new-found overwhelming sense of shame.

And I realize why I recognize this guy. I *am* this guy. Although I never beat up my lover's lover. He was off to Tahiti with my wife before I ever knew what happened. I only ever got to beat up myself. This probably felt good for him. Pounding the man who you can only assume did the worst to his one true love, the woman he married, the mother of his children, the pride of his island. And I'm the asshole that did that worst. I'm the asshole that seduced his wife and got her drunk and gave her psychedelic drugs and told her I loved her and though never in words but in kindred thoughts promised her a life away from her life, if she wanted it. If she wanted *me*. And who knows, maybe she still does. If she's not in the back of the shanty there, fixing Thanksgiving dinner, laughing at my stupidity. Or maybe she's out there somewhere, searching for me on her own adventure the way I'm searching for her here, circling the resort, possibly seeing all those people in the lobby and now she's assuming the worst, that I have left her, when maybe she is ready for me to save her from all of this after all. Perhaps this was what all those nervous looks added up to, the fear that I would leave before she had a chance to tell me how she felt. Maybe this is why she left without a word this morning, not because she doesn't love me. She had to get out of there before she was seen, or even more importantly before she was missed by her family. Hell, maybe she just had to go home and feed her kids?

The door opens. He's come back for more. "Stay back," he tells the kids, and the same grit that's in the palms of my hands squishes under his boot until he stands over me. Something cool drips over my leg.

"Stand up."

"I don't think I can."

He kneels over me, offering a cool glass of water, and a warm, wet kitchen towel.

I take it and drink. Then gulp. I down the whole thing, and then take the towel. I wipe my face first, covering the towel in blood. It ain't pretty. I fold it and wipe again, gingerly, as every piece of cartilage in my face is tender, and then scrub my hands.

"You okay?"

"I think it's ruined." I'm talking about my shirt. He knows what I really mean. My ego. My chances. He looks off, catching the eye of the old woman on the lawn. She stares back at us, unmoved by the experience. He nods to the old lady, a casual courteous acknowledgment that he sees her, with a recognition that she, too, sees him, with no words exchanged.

Mena's husband rings the rag out, then tosses the soggy red linen in the cup. He reaches his strong tatted arm down and helps me to my feet. I stand, stiffly, and dust myself off. Despite the buzz cut Mohawk and all the tattoos, this guy could be a fitness model. He's super cut, and, ass-whipping aside, seems like a super-chill surfer-bro.

"Thanks." I mean for helping me up, not the ass-whooping. Although maybe I deserved that, too.

"There's a story on this island, the story of Maui, the son of Ru, who wanted nothing more than to separate the heavens from the Earth. See, when Maui was a boy, the only thing separating the sky from the Earth were plants, their leaves squished flat from trying to hold up the other world, and this pressure was suffocating for the people of the Islands. With the heavens bearing down on them so closely it was impossible to move about, and thus Maui decided to make a change and lift the Heavens from the Earth, if only he could figure out how. He knew that this change would allow people to be able to walk tall, and the trees would grow freely, and the Earth would flourish. Then one day he fortuitously met a woman and he told that woman what he planned to do and asked if she would give him some warm soup so that he might have the energy to lift the sky away from the Earth. And, after contemplating his request, she gave him a taste from her gourd calabash. Upon tasting the soup, Maui was filled with new life, and he proceeded to push the sky from the ground below, all the way up the mountain until they were over the highest peaks of Haleakala, and beyond the Seven Pools of Ohe'o. And it was backbreaking work, but he did it, and the people of the island rejoiced his success. And now, because of his efforts and the kindness of the old woman, the skies of the island are clear and sunny, and the heavens no longer suffocate the people of Earth the way they once did. But, every once and again, a storm blows in, and Maui has to remind the Heavens of his great and wonderful power by blowing them back out again. But it never stops them from trying. I suppose in nature, like life, a storm is always brewing."

I stare at him in silence. I have no idea what he's talking about. Not because I wasn't trying to pay attention, but because the only thing I can concentrate on right now is the throbbing of my brain inside my skull and a tingling sensation in the side of my face. He searches me for a reaction, a response of any kind, some sort of tell that I was paying attention, and all I know is I can physically feel my lip swelling like an inflating party balloon.

"Do you need a ride?"

You've got to be kidding me. First I fuck his wife. Then he beats the shit out of me. Then I get a history lesson about the legend of the sky, and now, what? A *ride*? *Really? Who is this guy?*

"If you don't mind."

What other option do I have?

The next thing I know I'm riding shotgun in a pickup truck, Mena's husband at the wheel, and their two kiddos, the big one holding the little one in his lap between us. I'm pretty sure on the mainland this is illegal, but I don't feel I'm in a very strong position to question him at the moment. He's got a pretty stern look on his face, but I think we're cool.

He drops me back at the hotel, and with a polite wave, he's off. I don't want to see anybody here, not the Samoan concierge, not Ken, not anyone, so I whisk around back in sight of only the valet, who immediately calls someone on his walkie. I'd have to be paranoid or narcissistic to think he's calling about me, but I can't help it. I always do.

I slip through a side entrance by the gardens and weave my way back to the room. I need to leave here, pronto. Any premonitions I might have had that Mena would leave him for me are purely delusional. She's got two kids, for Christ's sake. I was just... a mistake.

And that's the real reason she left this morning. I get that now. But still, if there was some way I could convince her that this is all worthwhile, I would. That the adventurous life she was looking for, that the escape she needs to feel alive and fulfilled, I can bring her that, if only she'll give me the chance. But I know better. And I begin to pack.

It doesn't take long; I don't bring much. I keep my bags organized. A product of regular traveling. I take a two-minute shower and raid the minie-fridge one last time in hopes that nobody filled it from my last raid so it will still be on the magazine's dime. You never know when you'll get hungry during a flight. Plus, I know I've already missed my flight to LAX so I'll have to take whatever's available. Better to have some chips, peanuts, and chocolate on hand in case there's a delay and I end up in some rinky-dink airport for twelve hours. And if I can somehow still make my deadline in time I won't even have to pay.

I carry my luggage to the door and say farewell to my luxurious bedroom, leave the keys on the bed, close the door, and make my way down the hall to the front. Bill, the cheerful Samoan concierge, nods politely as I exit, suitcases scrolling behind me. I feel a sense of relief. This is all about to be over. This ridiculous thing I've gotten myself into is finally going to end. Well, good riddance. Feelings or no feelings, this is turning out to be a fiasco.

The glass doors breeze open around me and I can feel the warm wind against my face. The valet stands there, next to the taxi stand, watching me as I hesitantly make my way over, then stop. A curious look on his face as I turn myself inward to confront my true feelings before I do something drastic and stupid.

But what are my true feelings? I really do love her, right? And what if, just by some stretch of the imagination she feels it, too? What if she's out there, right now, looking for me like I'm looking for her? She could be, I know it. Just like I've known about her this whole time. What we had last night was undeniable. What we have between us, this is real. And if I walk out this door right now, I will never know. I'll never know how she feels or what our future could be like. I will never know if I had a shot or not, and I will never know if all of these feelings are just in my head, or are they real, for both of us? I'll never know if I am just some mistake in a long line of mistakes that's lodged itself between her and her husband. And I can't live not knowing. So, embarrassment be damned, I turn around determined to find her at all costs when I quickly realize I've just locked the keys inside my hotel room after raiding the minie-fridge and calling the front desk to check out. *Damn.*

But there, in the back of my head is the tiniest spark of an idea about where I can find Mena, and I race to get out of there as fast as I can.

I roll my bags over to Bill, the smiling Samoan concierge. Bill doesn't appear so happy to see me anymore.

"Aloha." I offer.

He looks me over. No doubt the swelling of my face and the blackening beneath my eyes are a real turnoff.

"Hi."

"Can I, uh… ask you a favor?"

"If you like."

"Do you have, like, a bag check or anything?"

"Yes, sir. You can leave your bags with me if you like. I'll make sure they're put safely away in our storage closet."

I eagerly leave my bags and my briefcase behind and zoom off. Out the back exit, down the little pathway, I glance over my shoulder for the briefest of seconds just to get a glimpse of the old tiki hut as I race down the boardwalk that separates the sandy oceanfront from the developed land of the resorts.

I take off down the beach, unsure of where I'm going, having only the faintest impression that if there is anywhere in the world I might find her, it will be someplace she knows she can be alone. A place she goes when she wants to escape.

I don't remember where it is, exactly, but I know what I'm looking for. The night we ate all of the mushrooms she took me there, her special place, where you can look up through the canopy of the earth into galaxies unexplored on the other side. I race down the beach, blindly, my mind strobing back to that night, that vibrating pulsating night with the music of my soul filling me up like the infinite stars in the pitch-black sky.

And then I'm standing there. In her special spot. I look up. The sun is blinding. My eyes water with tears and I am forced to look away, back into the shadows to dispel my patchwork vision. The sun freckles the ground with dancing rays of light, but the hammock is empty.

"Mena?" I ask.

I turn around. I know she's here. I can feel it. I was drawn here by her. By her being. By our oneness. I know where she is and I know what she's thinking and right now she's whispering in my ear and saying "I'm scared."

I turn and she's there. Sitting behind a tree, shaded by the overgrown palms above, facing the cozy little beach house whose owners hung this calming little hammock. I thought she owned this place originally. Come to find out this place isn't hers at all. Nothing is hers. And yet, everything.

"What are you scared of?"

131

"What happens next."

I grin. I knew if I followed my instincts they would lead me here, and now all I want to do is reassure her and let her know that I'm here to stay and the hard part is over, and now we can finally be together, forever. I sit beside her.

"Don't you have a plane do catch?"

I'm at a loss.

"How did you know?"

"I work in a hotel, Frank. Everybody knows everything."

"Oh. Well... I skipped it."

"What for?"

She looks at me, uncertain. She's more callow than I thought. I search her eyes for meaning behind the blooming petals of sadness.

"I had to see you first."

"Oh." She wipes a gloop of snot, clumping in her nose. I long for a smile, but she looks away instead. Back into the sand, a million miles away.

"You ever wake up and look around at everything you have, everything you've accomplished, everything you are and everything you'll never become and realize your life won't ever amount to shit?"

"No."

"You never thought, like, what if I disappeared, right here and right now, would anyone even care? Would anyone even notice? Would it even matter? Or would life just go on, the way it always does? With or without me?"

I don't have time for this shit. Why does she always waste time with this shit? We've got things to discuss. Important things. So many things I don't know where to start, so I cut right to the chase.

"I met your husband."

She looks at me. "I can see that."

"Why didn't you tell me?"

"Why would I?"

I shrug. Good question. She always asks good questions. I try one.

"What now?"

She stands up. "Why are you here, Frank?"

"I wanted to see you."

"No. Why are you here? Why are you on this island?"

"I…" My mind goes blank. Out of all the things she could have asked, it's the question I'm least prepared for.

"What was the plan, huh? Find some local chick to hook up with so you could have some cool story to tell your work buddies when you get home? Go on some sort of adventure, like you said?"

I look at her aghast. I can't believe she'd even think that.

"No. Of course not."

"Then what?"

She thinks I'm lying. All she wants is a confession so she can lop my head off and feed me to the sharks. She thinks I just came here and used her. For *sex*. Like some kind of *whore*. How long she's thought that and her complicity in the matter is irrelevant. *I* am the perpetrator. *She* is the victim.

It's time for the truth. The whole truth. And nothing but the truth. The truth will set you free. The truth, and then we can finally live happily ever after, just as we've intended all along. The truth is so much better than whatever she's concocted in her head, that this was all planned, premeditated in some way to trick her, and now she's just the victim of my Lothario plot. No, this is fate. This is *destiny*. This is Heaven and Earth shifting around us night after night to place us together so that we will come together, unite as one, and be soul mates.

"Why are you here?" She demands. She's prepared herself for the absolute worst, and all I have to do is be truthful.

"The tournament."

"What? What tournament?"

"The basketball tournament. I was hired by some stupid website to write about it."

She stares at me, inconclusively. "Huh?"

"I'm a writer. That's why I'm here."

She looks astonished. Somehow, this awful truth of my existence pains her even worse than it does me. Somehow it pains her worse than any other emotional sword I have already stabbed her with.

"Jesus Christ. Are you kidding me?"

"No. Why?"

She looks aghast. "When you said you *loved* me I thought you were just trying to get in my pants! I didn't know you were *serious*! I thought you were, like, some kind of entrepreneur or something, here for the convention. Some sort of smooth-talking salesman or something. Isn't that what you said?"

I remember saying nothing of the sort, but how could I remember? I've been drunk, drugged or high practically the entire time I've been here.

"So, wait... You're a *writer*?" She needs more clarity. The truth isn't enough.

"I'm *kind of* an entrepreneur."

She scoffs. "Puh-lease. How old are you anyway?"

"Forty-three."

Her jaw falls open and her eyebrows peel back across her forehead in horror.

"Forty-three? Are you fucking kidding?"

"I wish."

"I thought you were like, thirty-two. Thirty-five, max."

I grin from ear to ear. That's the best news I've heard in ages.

"Really? That's awesome. How old are you?"

"Twenty-four."

Hold the phone.

"Wait... You're how old?"

"Twenty-four. Why? How old did you think I was?"

Thirty-four? I dunno, but I can't say that. I know better than to go there.

"Twenty-five or six. Maybe a couple years older."

Whew. Dodged a bullet on that one.

"You're disgusting."

Or, maybe not. My clueless expression gives me away dead to rights.

"You're just like everybody else." She throws her shoulder bag around her and takes off.

Like a masochist, I plead for more.

"What do you mean?"

She stops in her tracks and turns. I stare at her dumbly as she looks at me, pinning me squarely in my place for whatever she's about to hurl my way.

"Seriously, Frank? You walk around like some smart-ass know-it-all like you've got it all figured it out, throwing money around like you own the world, when really, you're just some sad little puppy, still starving for Mommy's attention, just like every other asshole I know. You're forty-three years old, man. Grow up. It's fucking pathetic."

I'm lost in my own thoughts. Blinded by my own feelings. Betrayed by my own words. I call out, helplessly.

"But, didn't you have fun?"

She chortles at the thought.

"Of course I had fun. I didn't fall in *love*."

She backs away and as she turns to face new horizons I can't help wonder if that last bit was for me, to make me feel even worse than I already do, or for her, to make her feel better. Probably both. There are too many questions left unanswered, and even more feelings and emotions jumbling up my head, but there's one thing that's crystal clear to me now: there's no reason to chase her anymore. There's no reason to tell her how I feel. There's no reason to do anything at all in this whole entire world except lie down. So, I pull the hammock open and do just that.

*   *   *   *   *

At some point, it must have rained. I wake up to the tiny pitter-patter of raindrops on my face, dripping down my cheeks, and my shirt is soaked. Right across my chest, like my shrunken and shriveled heart has squeezed out the last remaining goop from inside, and there it sits, a dark wet stain on my soul.

She's right. I am just like everyone else. The assholes, the gel heads, the mouth breathers, and super fans. I am them and they are me. Only worse. I've spent an entire life going and doing and trying and being and living and barely scraping by only to be in the exact same place I've always been, all by myself. Where does the time go? What exactly have I been doing with it?

And now, after all that time spent wasted, now that I thought I had it all figured out... That She... That *It*... That *This* could save Us. That *This* could save Me. *This*, which surrounds us and carries us and moves us, every one of us, and fills us with life and lust and emotional fulfillment to make us whole and enlightened beings before our desperate pursuit for happiness ends, leaving us right back where we started.

This which is *Love*.

But now she is gone, and all that remains of *This* is a tired black hole, sucked into itself with nothing left but the sustained agony of heartbreak. The world is over. There is nothing else. Just this blackened heart and the hardening of my dry clay soul.

I haven't cried in ages, the well's gone dry after years of emotional repression and alcohol. So now, in lieu of crying, my tear ducts dry heave, retching my gut forward in violent thrusts until finally something wet spurts out across my cheek. I squeeze my eyelids tight, the thought of her naked over top of me, smiling, her kids through the screen door, gawking, her husband driving silently through the overcast afternoon, angry, floods my mind. My head's still kind of throbbing, but it's Thanksgiving afternoon and I'm in a hammock in Paradise crying my eyes out and all I can think of is her. The one true woman in my life. The only woman I ever really loved and the only woman I probably ever will.

Not Mena. My ex-wife. The mother of my unborn children. Purveyor of my sun, my moon, my everything, the woman of which after first laying eyes on her, I knew we would never part. I was mostly right. For a long time, at least. And then, I think what happens to everyone happened to us. The kid thing, of course, was a blow. Her more than me. But that's a woman's right. She couldn't have them and I said I didn't care, but I think she felt bad about that. I think she never got over it. And the book, well, the book was a disaster. I don't know what I was thinking. And then she was gone. And it was like suddenly a limb I had been favoring my whole life had been ripped out from under me and I had to learn to walk all over again. And I was numb, and bloody, and scarred from where the limb had torn, and I hoped for a long time that it would regenerate in purpose, in being, in a physical manifestation… but it was too late then, and it's too late now. I have only what I am left with on this journey, like all others before it: myself, and myself to blame.

I stare at my reflection in the cloudy sky and wonder what I could have done differently. For either of them. For anybody. For everybody. Throughout my entire life. I think of anyone and everyone I ever lied to, wronged, or selfishly misguided, and the list is exhausting. *I am a terrible person* I surmise at the end of it, no longer quivering in fear of being alone and the pain I've caused myself and others, but growing pale with exhaustion, self-loathing, and disgust. There is nothing more I can do. There is no more to do. There is no more to say. There is nothing. Love is an illusion. Betrayal a foregone conclusion. Lust is your enemy, an enticing lure on a hook that will snag you right between the lips and leave you cold and flopping on someone else's cutting board. All that's left once the love is gone is death.

I sit up, dizzy like I've been hit with more than her husband's fistful of truth, more like a sledgehammer of it, right across my face. I haven't felt this seasick since Hana. Or *The Road To*. I look out, staring off into the vast ocean as the dark clouds roll out to sea. The waves are rougher than usual, pounding the unforgiving beach with greater force than before, gnashing and gnawing away at it with foamed mouth, but the beach stands firm, bracing for the abuse with its tempered skin as the water breaks over it and draws back into itself again.

The frothy waves roll out over the sand like a blanket pulling itself snugly up and over the ground to cover it before sliding back out, slipping across the earth like a satin robe, back into the sea where it collects all the trash and scum and leftovers of the wasteland with it. And as the tide washes in, like in my hallucination before, the waves roll out over the ocean to form an escalator of water charging into the sky. The sun is blocked behind the clouds, but the faintest glimmer of hope shines through, suggesting the possibility of a new dimension and a path toward salvation on the other side. This is finally it, I think as I am pulled by the current from my seat, that moment of enlightenment I've been seeking this entire trip only a moment away if I can only rise up on these outlaid stairs across the horizontal plains of the sea and transcend my state of being into a heavenly body that promises to finally set me free.

I am slowly enveloped, teased at first with a lap and a sprinkle until I fall waist-deep into the water, no longer a dry pillar wading into the sun, but a battered sea vessel, whipped up by a current of monstrous waves in front of me before I am completely overtaken into darkness.

At least it's warm. Warmer than I would have expected on this cool, windy, overcast day. And I'm enveloped, drawn under the ravaging waves above into a perfect submarine calm along the sandy ocean floor. And I have long forgotten about the stairway to salvation and can now only think about the depravity and despair of my being, and the pathway toward hell, which I am no doubt heading toward. She was right, after all, I am totally pathetic.

Yet even realizing this, I find myself at peace. I am back in the womb of my mother's belly. Her nurturing fluid surrounding me, enveloping my wrinkled hands and my curved little feet. I can hear the beating rhythm of her slow and steady heart, coursing through her loving soul. And now my lungs, my blood, and my body, they are given back over to nature until the only thing left flowing through me is a feeling of eternal stillness. And it is only now that I realize that afterward, this is it. There is no more. There is no Other. There is only that which came before. And I am finally able to answer Mena's riddle from earlier. Once we are gone, we are gone forever.

I drown in the realization that I'm not ready to be gone forever. Or maybe I'm just drowning.

"UHHHH!!!" I open my eyes, ears, and mouth, gasping for breath, only I suck in nothing but water. I cough, immediately, as another wave crashes over me and I realize I do not want to die. Not here. Not now. Not ever. I don't care if I was making plans to change my life and now those plans are crashing down on me like a tidal wave in the sea. I want to live. And if I don't get out of here, like, *now*, I won't. I thrash, wildly, hoping, praying to find my way out of this salty death trap, but it's hopeless. The only thing I feel is the blackness sucking the life out of me as the air in my lungs is quickly replaced by water.

I feel something against my arm. Something hard, tugging me. It's not over yet. There's either a rescue afoot or I'm about to be torn to shreds by a savage shark. I kick at it to scare it away, then it's around my waist, grabbing me, dragging me desperately to shore.

I'm flipped on my back but I can't see anything. There are only sounds.

"Is he okay?"

"What happened?"

"He just... walked out there."

"What was he doing?"

"I saw this guy yesterday."

"Can he swim?"

"Please, get back!"

And then something bangs on my chest, shattering the rib that was already cracked, along with the two on either side of it. They put their mouth to mine, and after sucking and blowing, sucking and blowing, I come alive, spitting water all over their face as I shoot upright. I clunk my giant noggin right against their lead jaw.

"Are you okay, sweetheart?"

I open my eyes... hoping... expecting...

It's the Queen. And he's got his shirt off, of course. Flexing for the entire crowd. He's got great abs, there's really no doubt. And he did just save my life.

I gasp for breath, still choking, apologizing profusely. "I'm so sorry."

"It's alright. You'll be okay."

He kneels beside me and helps me up. One of his friends hands him a towel and he wraps it around me.

"Thanks," I mutter. It doesn't sound as heartfelt as I want, but I'm still trying to catch my breath.

He nods, hugs me against him, and helps me up, dusting the sand from my soaking wet pants. He always was a little handsy.

"You need to watch yourself, sport. Undertow's strong today."

"I can tell."

He gives me a stern look.

139

"You gotta take better care of yourself, darling. Know your limits. Understand your environment. Otherwise... you know. If you can't swim you shouldn't jump in the ocean."

"No... I can swim." It sounds like I'm making excuses.

The small crowd stares back at me like it's open mic night at the local comedy club. Their concern pierces through me like a stern parent glares at their child. I know I've fucked up. Here and elsewhere. Before and now. And I can't help but know with certainty I will fuck up again. But maybe next time it won't be quite so monumental.

"You'll be okay. I think maybe you just need some rest."

"That sounds like an excellent idea."

I hand him his friend's towel back. My ribs are killing me. I offer my hand, and he shakes it, a firm, hardy shake. Not at all what I expected. I'm so fucking judgmental.

"Thanks for saving my life."

"Anytime, partner. You come back later I'll give you a little swimming lesson, on the house."

He grins, playfully, and I wearily trudge sopping wet back through the sand to the hotel for no other reason than my luggage is there. There's nothing else for me there. There's nothing for me anywhere, along this beach or across this island. I've worn out my welcome. The signs are more than clear, it's time for me to leave.

And this sand. I freaking hate this sand. The way it sticks to you when you're wet. Clinging to your pants and climbing up your underwear and into your crawl. Or the way it gets into your socks, seeping into the corners of your shoes until you rub blisters on your feet. It's impossible to maneuver without exhausting yourself in the stuff, but I finally make it back, panting like a wet dog.

I head inside, walking right through to reception, wet shoes squishing across the tile floor, squeaking with each and every step. I can feel the eyes of every employee on me as I lumber through the lobby. It's a small island. Word travels fast. Or maybe I'm paranoid. Either way, I lose.

I've already missed my flight, but surely there's another. It doesn't matter where. San Francisco. San Diego. Taiwan. Anywhere but here. Here or home.

I see Bill behind the front desk and I greet him with a false smile.

"Hi, I checked some baggage with you earlier."

"Do you have a ticket?"

I check for a ticket. I can't find a ticket. There was no ticket. He never gave me a ticket.

"You never gave me one."

The Samoan stares at me with nothing but contempt. Now I've offended him, personally.

"What is your name, sir?"

Is this a trap? Is he entering me into the system, permanently, so that I won't be able to travel anywhere ever again without being labeled as difficult? He's already got my name, anyway, from before. Is this some sort of a test?

"Frank Shaw."

He types something. It seems a lot longer than F-R-A-N-K—S-H-A-W. Oh shit, maybe he *is* calling someone. Alerting someone. Messaging someone… about *me*! But what have I done exactly? What does he know? He pops a drawer behind the counter and swipes out a ring full of keys.

"Right this way."

I follow him down a hallway full of doors. I've seen this movie before. It didn't end well for the guy who played me. And then, he stops, studying one of the doors before inspecting the key ring. He carefully slides each key aside as he considers what it might be used for until he finally chooses one. He inserts it into the slot, but it doesn't fit. He tries the next one, it doesn't fit either. He looks at me, nervously.

"What are we doing here?"

He's inspecting the keys again when suddenly, he's got it. He tries the key in the slot and the third time's a charm. The lock pops and the door swings open and the Samoan eagerly ushers me inside.

It's dark. I can't see a thing. The fluorescent lights finally pop on. I'm standing in a narrow storage closet full of suitcases.

"Are any of these yours?"

Ohhh-kayyyy. Well, first off, they all look the same. And secondly, I have no idea what mine even looks like. I didn't put any defining features on it, it's just a black, zip-up suitcase.

"Hard case of soft? Rollers or Carry?"

It's like he's reading my mind.

"Hard case, rollers."

He starts sorting through them and quickly grabs a bright yellow one.

"Black."

He sets it down, rummaging through the rest.

I stand as if supervising the expedition but with a wandering eye I admire some of the others in here. There's a $1,400 Louis Vuitton piece, next to the $2,600 one. What if I tell him that's mine, I wonder what I'll find inside? Or maybe a smaller more discreet one? What are the chances I'll find money in it? Jewelry? Or something else of value?

Or what if beneath all that expensive stitching and fancy embroidery the inside is vacant. Or worse. Three hundred dollar jeans. Three thousand dollar sundresses. Void of purpose beyond the expression of vanity, and no more useful than a sale rack cotton blend from a big box store or a free hand-me-down from a friend. Which one am I, I wonder? The utilitarian cotton bud, stretched and pulled into dyed threads to be woven together to provide privacy and comfort at an affordable cost to mankind, or am I an elaborate, pretentious garment that demands value much greater than my worth, forcing myself upon my clientele with petty promises that will tatter, fade, and tear on a zipper in the spin cycle of the laundry load of life just like everything else you throw in the washer.

"I don't see it."

I concur, unhappily. I should have claimed the LV. At least I could have sold it.

"Come on." He draws me out of the closet as I take one more quick gander. I inspect more closely this time now that there's real potential for all my shit to be gone. He turns the light off, prompting me to give up, and I walk out into the hall. He locks the storage closet up then saunters back down the hall toward the front desk, where I line up opposite him once again.

"So, what now?"

"Well, it looks like your luggage has been misplaced."

"What does that mean, misplaced?"

The Samoan gets defensive.

"You were just back there with me. Did you see it? Because if you did…"

"You hardly gave me any time to look!"

"We were there for ten minutes. The closet isn't that big."

"Well, I've checked out already and I'm ready to leave. When do you expect to find it?"

"If you had a ticket it would be much easier."

"But that was your fault!"

"Sir, there's no reason to place blame on anyone. If you say you gave us your luggage, then we will locate your luggage. In the meantime, I can offer you a complimentary meal and two drinks in our dining room."

"I'm supposed to fly out any minute!" Lies. "I'm about to miss my flight because of you! This is fucking ridiculous!" A lie and an explicit-laden overstated truth.

"Well, sir, if you would like, we may be able to offer you a complimentary room for the night."

"Oh… You *may*…" I'm getting emboldened. Not necessarily because I want to stay any longer than I have to, but because they lost my friggin' luggage! I mean, c'mon man!

The Samoan goes to talk to some other guy, and I catch the looks between them. They aren't speaking kindly about me. *I've got a troublesome customer. He's blaming us for losing his luggage. He's the one that fucked the bartender with the husband and two kids.*

"I didn't know she was married, asshole!"

They look at me sternly. I bite my tongue. Maybe I should flee now while I still have the chance. Before they lock me up and throw away the key in some awful mobile prison they drive back and forth along the coast to Hana just to make the prisoners as sick as possible. What am I really losing here anyway? A couple suits. My electric razor and toothbrush. A bunch of stolen food and miniature liquor bottles from the minibar. Couple towels, robes, and slippers I stuck in the other day when I saw the maid's cart outside the room. I can probably get some more of those before I go.

Bill grabs something off the printer and as he approaches I stiffen. I missed my opportunity, and now must await the punishment for my crimes. The big guy settles across from me, his stomach pressing ever so gently into the counter in front of him as he holds out a new piece of paper.

"Alright, Mr. Shaw. We're prepared to offer you your old room for the night, as well as two complimentary meals at Aloha's, our signature restaurant, plus drink tickets. In the meantime, we will do what we can to locate your bag, and if you need any assistance with re-directing your travel plans, Margo over at our Travel and Destinations desk will be happy to help you." He hands me a receipt with all the numbers zeroed out and a genuinely polite smile.

"Yeah, thanks a lot."

I toss the papers back across the desk and stride off.

Damn, that felt good. But the sand up my crack and the raw chaffing of my underwear on my thighs is killing me. I've got to get out of here. But first, a bathroom.

I walk in and the scent of pineapple potpourri envelopes me, a sickeningly sweet smell that immediately reminds me of my grandmother, assuming my grandmother lived in Hawaii in her formative years and kept this type of potpourri around to remind her of her youth. Which she didn't. The farthest west she ever got was Arizona. But she did love pineapple.

I admire myself in the mirror. Not so much admire, really, as inspect. How the hell could she have deluded herself into thinking I was thirty-five? Look at me. I'm wrinkled. Hairy. Forlorn. What did a young girl like Mena ever see in a salty, saggy old bastard like me to begin with? I dunno… Maybe I'm too hard on myself. Even at my age, I'm in better shape than most, and so what if I'm a couple pounds overweight… it doesn't mean I'm fat. I just need to do better. I know that now, or at least I think I do. It was ridiculous to think we could be something. I'm ridiculous. I thought she was the one. I thought maybe she could love me. I thought I was in love with her. I think maybe I still am.

My mind is reeling. There are still so many things to say. So many fantasies unfulfilled. So many emotions, tangled up and confused. She had that tattoo on her back. That symbol, whatever it was. I meant to ask her about it. She probably thinks it means 'Paradise" or something. She probably doesn't even know what it means. That's the problem with getting symbols tattooed in a place you can't even see. It will forever remain a mystery, to me and to her. And now we will never know, together.

*   *   *   *   *

The taxi ride reminds me of her. The palm trees remind me of her. The ocean reminds me of her. Everything reminds me of her, for better or worse, through sickness and in health. I don't know how many hours I've slept this week, but it doesn't feel like much, and I'm exhausted. My soul is exhausted. My inner well-being, as well as just about everything on the outside, too, is exhausted. And I'm still wet, even though I sat under the air dryer in the men's room until a circuit blew before dabbing myself off with every paper towel I could get out of the dispenser. I considered trying the women's, but it was occupied. I pass the skycap at the airport and grimace with the memory of my lost luggage. It's not the only thing I'm leaving behind on this trip. And what very little I've gained.

The airport is dead. Everyone left already. There aren't a lot of flights out at this time of night. None, really, except the one to LA that leaves at 5:15. Tomorrow morning. Ugh. I buy the ticket and take a seat. The dampness of my wardrobe slowly seeps into my skin, the whole lot of me gradually beginning to mildew.

God, I miss her. I feel like we could have had everything in the world, if only we tried. Not my wife. Mena. My wife's been gone for years. She was gone before she ever really left, and after that it was only a matter of time before she was gone for good. I had begged. Pleaded. For years this persisted, for what only felt like months. Until finally, she broke. It wasn't me, she told me one time, but I knew it wasn't true. How can it *not* be you when before the affair you were all there was and you were all that was needed and you were more than enough. To lose her, not to a car accident or to disease or to any type of mortal fate, but to someone else, that was excruciatingly painful and had deeply scarring effects. Effects that I have buried and maybe am only just finally beginning to realize and understand for the very first time. The pain within cuts deep, still burning through the belly in powerful waves, like an internal hemorrhaging of the soul, and a continuous outpouring of life, draining you of all resources you ever had or had left to give. And there is no way to let it all out except to purge it, bleed it dry, puncturing the nerve deep within, wriggling it free from the hardwired mainframe and slowly massaging it back to life, one stroke at a time, until that tiny essence that once was, like the re-germination of a hardened root, grows new tendrils of spirit and renewed blossoms of character, and with time and partnership and tender nurturing it eventually sprouts again into a new love.

But not today.

Today I need to deliver something, *anything*, to my publisher, in less than fourteen hours, or I have to pay for this whole God-forsaken trip myself and I don't even have a computer. I can barely keep my eyes open. I just need to get some rest.

6
Friday

I lurch in my seat to the announcement. I'm looking for her, but she's not here. I'm looking for anyone I might recognize, but there's only the blur of unrecognizable faces of the people still standing in line, waiting to get on. The seat next to me is empty. I can only hope it stays that way. I'm absolutely overtaken with exhaustion. I just don't have the energy for this life anymore. What's the point? Maybe I can just sleepwalk through it a little while longer. Nobody will know the difference. Nobody has so far. I can't help but close my eyes.

Someone brushes up against me as they move past, but I don't care. I'm out like a light. These first-class seats really are comfortable. Spacious. I could get used to this. I'd love to go to a tournament overseas somewhere where I could fly on one of those Dreamliner things. One of those cool planes with a whole bed. And a TV in the headrest in front of you. That would be nice. If I ever get another job again. My deadline is rapidly approaching and I can't help but crawl into a nap. Fortunately, I was able to buy a laptop off some kid in the terminal for six hundred bucks, and he even let me keep the software.

Just about the time I'm settling into a dreamlike state the steward comes over the loudspeaker to make his boarding announcements. I thrash awake like I'm falling from 10,000 feet, startling the woman in fur who's taken her seat next to me. I apologize silently and look up where I catch the eye of a surprisingly cute stewardess adjusting the luggage overhead.

"Would you like a cocktail or something to drink? Bloody Mary? Mimosa?" She offers them up with a glint in her eye.

Even if it wasn't 5 a.m. the urge does not suit me. I politely decline.

"I'll have one. Mimosa please." I look at the woman in fur, my eyes slowly adjusting to the soft, fuzzy image before me when it hits, she's a fox. I don't mean to stare, my reflexes are just slow, and now I swear she keeps glancing at me. She probably thinks I'm staring. I look away once more. I've got other things to think about. Like her. How much I'm going to miss her, even if it was only a few nights. I guess we'll always have Paradise.

I chuckle at my own stupid joke and she smiles at me. I never really understood that silly saying until now. It's cheesy but it's true. This adventure, for better or worse, will definitely stay with me forever. I guess Mena would be happy to know that memories don't really die like I thought while I was drowning, not the important ones. The important ones live on forever, as long as we share them with others. It's how legends are born. It's how history is made. Perhaps if we all make wiser decisions we will lead ourselves toward a fuller, richer future. But we won't.

About the time I get my seat buckled the male steward finishes with the safety demo and we start taxiing down the runway. I bounce unpleasantly in my seat. This plane needs better shock absorbers. And my seat is way too big and cushy. I wonder what the passengers in back feel. I used to be one of those. Still am, really. I'm a faker up here. I'm a faker everywhere I go, apparently. Faking it like I've got it together. Shit, I don't have it together. I'm a mess. Constantly overcompensating.

For lack of purpose. Lack of training. Fear of failure. Fear of success. Only I thought maybe I had finally found that purpose again, a reason to continue, but like the infinitesimal grains of sand in a cracked hourglass, it sifted from my fingers and left me an empty vessel once more.

I look toward the window and catch the eye of the starry-eyed Vixen with her square sunglasses and furry jacket again, but she looks away, so I do, too. I look past her, out the window and down the sharp edge of the wing, out toward the watery horizon as all the definition blurs past in our eager acceleration across the tarmac. As we await the moment of lift-off, that moment when we reach that miraculous ability to pull ourselves out of the dirt, out of the gritty congested terrain and into the brilliant light of the sky, the tension between us peaks and without warning but through instinctual synchronicity the Vixen looks back at me, and I look back at her, and we smile at each other, and so it begins.

My heart pounds full of adrenaline. My body courses with excitement as we lift off, reeling in that moment between earth and sky when the gravitational forces that would normally hold you down are broken through and your ability to fly is restricted only by the amount of baggage you're carrying and your ability to gain momentum along the way. I sit back with these realizations as they penetrate me to my core, and I look out, squinting through the tiny oval window that separates us, the passengers, from free-falling like human rain out of the sky.

At first, I see nothing. Blue on blue. Waves on sky. One layer atop the other as the plane banks a hard left to change course. But now I can see everything. The mountains. The sugar cane fields. Black Rock. The other islands of Hawai'i. And the turquoise ocean as it expands toward the horizon in a navy-blue oblivion.

This truly is some kind of Paradise. I'm not sure what kind, exactly, but look at it. I close my eyes as I feel the energy of the islands surging through my veins. We plow through dense ocean air, the g-forces pulling against my taut skin, and suddenly I consider this space I'm in, between Heaven and Earth, the space that Maui created for us, for all of mankind to soar. And here I am, admiring it all through a tiny oval window in a giant aluminum cylinder as it hurdles me four hundred miles an hour along the edge of the ocean before finally leveling off over the sea.

Brilliant energy washes over me from the bright morning sunlight peeking in through my oval lookout. Blinding white light erases the mind's eye of right and wrong and love and hate and that which matters and that which doesn't to make room for a whole new creation. I can feel myself shedding my epidermal layer of baggage as it's replaced with the feeling of a whole new beginning. A new zest for life. A path toward opportunity. A path toward hope.

The cosmos surrounds me, filling me with vitality, firing through my blood, the tempo of my heart increasing as this electronic pulse wave courses through my body, and I realize that I if I am to overcome that which haunts me, I need to first overcome that which stands in my way: myself. And with this acknowledgment an overwhelming tidal wave of emotion floods back into my spirit after days, weeks, months, and years of burying myself in self-doubt and self-pity and fear of rejection and fear of success and personal guilt and repression and anger and obsession and madness about everything else in the world that I could never control and everything that I could that always made me feel helpless and worthless and unwanted. But pathetic no more, I create my own destiny. I await no man, or woman, to lure me with desire. I desire but one thing, that which I have always desired, and that which I always will. Life.

With fuel in my fire, I draw the teenager's laptop from its stickered case and slice into the keys with my gnawed bony fingertips. My mind is racing, flooding with ideas. The Assignment. The Assignment. The Assignment. I've got a day I tell myself. And a long plane ride ahead.

I tell her I'm on vacation I type hastily onto the screen. *Vacation sounds more like adventure. Work is like... well, you know what it's like...*

The words pour out of me with such intensity I'm unaware what's being written until I read it back across the page. My fingers slap across the keys with such veracity the Vixen sitting next to me can't help but watch. That clicking sound, the sound of feelings

150

forming into ideas as they spring into the mind, half-thought but constantly developing until they're typed into words on the page that flow with such efficiency that they create a subtle music, that melody of a tale just dying to come out, I relent myself to it. I don't know where I'm going or what I'm doing, but I know where I've been and that's as good as any place to start.

Thank you for reading "The Fabulist." If you enjoyed it, please consider telling your friends or posting a quick review on Amazon. Word of mouth and positive reviews are the absolute best ways for readers like you to help independent authors like me reach a wider, more engaged audience. Your help is greatly appreciated.

Thank you for all of your support!

~SWR

About the Author

Samuel W. Reed is a novelist, screenwriter, and film director from Paducah, Kentucky. He currently lives with his wife and children in Los Angeles, California.

For more information about
books, films, giveaways
& promotions, visit:

www.samuelwreed.com

twitter/instagram
@samuelwreed

facebook
@samuelwrite

Further reading from

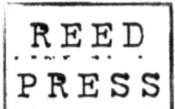

- **The Fabulist** - *Samuel W. Reed* (2017)

- **Miscreants, Murderers, & Thieves**: a collection of short stories about devious behavior - *Various* (2020)

- **Dirtbag** - *Samuel W. Reed* (Coming Soon)

- **Miscreants, Murderers, & Thieves II**: a deviant collection of murderous tales - *Various* (Coming Soon)

www.ingramcontent.com/pod-product-compliance
Lightning Source LLC
Chambersburg PA
CBHW051948170626
46808CB00007B/2532